Gotcha!

Gotcha!

L. D. Alan

Gotcha
© 2010 Linda D. Delgado All Rights Reserved

ISBN 978-0-9819770-5-8

Muslim Writers Publishing
PO Box 27362
Tempe, Arizona 85285

Book and Cover Design by Leila Joiner
Book Editing by Debora McNichol

Printed in the United States of America

This book is dedicated to all the honorable men and women who took the oath of office to *Serve and Protect.*

L. D. Alan

Rainey Walker Series Titles

Catch Me If You Dare
Gotcha!

Look for the third book in the series,
The Last Victim, in the fall of 2011

Reader comments about *Catch Me If You Dare*,
the first book in the Rainey Walker Series:

"I enjoyed reading *Catch Me If You Dare* and would rec-
ommend it to others who enjoy realistic crime dramas. L.D.
Alan is clearly very familiar both with police work and the
American Muslim community, and writes about them with
authority….." and "I also liked the fact that the serial killer's
back story is not only timely, but plausible. The ending, with
its promise of more Rainey stories to come, was satisfying,
if open-ended. One thing I really liked about this book was
that even though it is about a brutal serial killer, most of the
gory details were left to the imagination, making it suitable
for a teenage audience as well as an adult one."

— Pamela K. Taylor

"I loved the fast pace of the entire plot, it was so sus-
penseful, specially the cliff hanger at the end. Now I really
can't wait for the next book!"

— Sadiyah Ali

"Author L. D. Alan, an experienced law enforcement officer, used behind-the-scenes knowledge to build a captivating suspense."

— Linda Jitmoud

"Nothing is as it appears in this murder mystery story told with a refreshing voice. With information from the case files detailed throughout and moving between the killer's thoughts to the law enforcement's plans, the story unfolds not unlike a crime investigation drama on television. Betrayal, hidden agendas and suspicion surface throughout the book adding to the suspense. The unexpected ending leaves the reader eager to read what happens in the next installment of this thrilling series."

— Saara A. Ali

"I just finished the book...can't wait for the next one! It wasn't a hard read, it flowed and it kept you reading and wanting to see what the next page had to expose! Wonderful imagination and just "realistic" enough to make the reader feel like it's probable which keeps readers interested!"

— Ramona Vazquez

Acknowledgments

I would like to thank the readers of the first Rainey Walker Series book, *Catch Me If You Dare*. Your enthusiastic comments and emails to me about the book and series encouraged me to push forward with writing and publishing this second book in the series, *Gotcha!* I am hoping all of you will enjoy it as well. I am continuing the series with writing the third book, *The Last Victim,* which is scheduled for publishing in late 2011.

Prologue

Rainey was frightened, shivering, and filled with dread. She heard the screaming and fought her way to consciousness through the fog induced by the sleeping pills she had taken. She clapped her hand over her mouth when she realized that, once again, it was her own screams from the relentless nightmare that awakened her. For months after Sara's death and the Scarf Killer's escape from Arizona, Rainey dreamed about that night in the hospital. Lieutenant Jerald had held her hands and said, "It's about Sara. Rainy, I don't know any other way to tell you this, but just give it to you straight. Sara got to your house, opened the front door, and the bomb SK planted exploded. I'm so sorry, Rainey, but Sara is gone."

Rainey had jerked her hands away from the lieutenant and covered her ears, screaming "No! No!" That's when everything went dark and Rainey had slipped into unconsciousness.

The week following Sara's death was still a blur. DC Britt had flown to Arizona on one of the FBI's private planes and had taken charge of everything. He made sure the closed casket of Sara's remains was flown back to her family for burial. He registered Rainey at a downtown Phoenix hotel, where she stayed until the preliminary paperwork on the bombing of her home was filed with the police department and the insurance company. Rainey had signed her name on the mountain of paperwork where DC told her to sign. He had tried to tell her about the captain, but Rainey was too angry and bitter to listen. She didn't care if Captain Jonah Daniels pulled through or not. DC didn't argue with her. Three days after the destruction of her grandparents' home and Sara's murder, Rainey traveled back to New York with DC. The FBI, with Sara's family, held a memorial service for Sara that was a blur in Rainey's memory.

Rainey never returned to work for the FBI. DC asked her to take more leave before making that decision, but Rainey was adamant. SK was still out there, somewhere, and Rainey vowed never again to be constrained by bureaucratic red tape. Six weeks after Sara's burial, Rainey visited the cemetery where Sara was buried. It was then that she made up her mind to go back to teaching and free-lance forensic consulting. It was then Rainey decided to prepare for the day she would meet SK again.

The sudden appearance of Jonah Daniels yesterday and his softly spoken words, "She's on the hunt in California. SK. I need your help," had triggered the nightmare that had slowly faded over the past year.

"Oh, Sara!" Rainey sobbed into her pillow as silent tears rolled down her cheeks.

The Past Catches Up
Wednesday

Rainey sat hunched over her desk piled with student exams to her right and a red ink pen in her left hand poised over one of the student's test. How long had she been staring blankly at the paper in front of her she didn't know. The incessant ringing of the phone startled her. She tensed and waited until she heard the machine pick up.

"We are unable to come to the phone right now. Leave your name and call back number."

"Rainey, DC Britt here. Call me. It's urgent. We need to talk."

Rainey heard the recording machine click and slowly released her breath. It wasn't him, Jonah, but hearing from DC Britt, the head of the FBI's Special Profiling Division was just as bad. She didn't want to talk to DC or the I-SID captain. She was through with the FBI and wanted to be left alone. She'd made that clear when she returned to FBI headquarters and turned in her ID card, badge, and weapon with her resignation.

Believing that the serial killer the Arizona media had dubbed as the *Scarf Killer* was over three thousand miles away from her New York City apartment on the 16th floor of a high-end security high rise did not make Rainey feel any safer. Sooner or later she expected SK to surface.

Rainey got up from the desk and walked to the floor to ceiling windows of the loft and looked out at the maze of buildings obliterating the skyline. At night, thousands of city lights offered a breathtaking view, but in the cold light of day, a thick, foul-smelling haze of pollution settled over the city, obscuring almost everything below her 16th floor apartment view.

Rainey turned from the window and her eyes swept the huge loft that had become her home. Not a door marred the openness of the apartment, but the chrome and glass modern furnishings were as cold as Rainey's frozen heart. The horrible loss of Sara had left an emptiness inside Rainey that time, turning her back on her FBI career, and isolating herself from her past life had not healed.

Rainey's nightmares were often flashes of the killer's last message to her, "Catch Me If You Dare" written in the killer's own blood on the wall of the home of one of the killer's intended victims. She wanted nothing to do with the FBI, the captain, or the hunt for this killer. Let the captain, a US Army Special Investigations Division officer and Interpol liaison, and the FBI go after this vicious killer. She didn't want involved in their investigation. She didn't trust them with good reasons. Capturing the killer would not bring Sara back, nor would it ease the guilt Rainey felt for her failure to catch the killer in Arizona.

Rainey continued to respond to consult requests dealing with the examination of bones for law enforcement, but the need for her police sketch artist skills had diminished with advanced composite technology. The new hand-held units allowed almost anyone with moderate training and a good eye to create a workable sketch. Rainey's work was confined to a laboratory, where she was comfortable and paid well for her expertise.

The phone rang again. Rainey didn't wait. She grabbed her purse and house key from the coffee table and fled the loft and the ringing phone.

Confrontation

Wednesday

Jonah let the phone ring until the voice message told him Rainey was not answering. He knew she was home because he had staked out the building after following her home the day before. Jonah was tired after standing watch all night and morning outside the apartment building. Sooner or later she had to leave her apartment and he could not take the chance of missing her.

Rainey...my God... Jonah thought of her stricken face and her mounting anger, her harsh words, "Move out of my way!" and the empty silence as she had turned away from him yesterday, walking stiffly to her car. She drove away without a backward glance. She had lost weight and her face was thinner. A few strands of grey now feathered her temples.

Would she ever forgive him? "It's not about you, Jonah!" he sneered at himself for his moment of weakness. I need her help and somehow I have to convince her that she is needed for the investigation. Confronting her in the parking lot was the wrong approach.

Jonah stared across the street and watched a security officer standing guard in front of the double doors reach out and open them. Rainey practically flew through the open doors without acknowledging the security officer. She turned left and jogged down the sidewalk, oblivious to the pedestrians coming from the opposite direction.

"Shit!" Jonah cursed softly and sprinted across the street, setting off a barrage of honking horns. He barely avoided a collision with a yellow cab as he made his way across the street and began following Rainey. He slowed his pace so he wouldn't overtake her while keeping a visual on her. *Was she headed for Central Park?*

After six blocks, Rainey turned right, still moving at a fast pace. *Yes…the park was just two blocks ahead of her now and nothing else.* Jonah slowed down, giving her time to get to the park and relax.

Rainey slowed her pace as she approached the park. Her breathing was ragged and a cold sweat had formed across her brow. The feeling of panic began to subside as she found an empty bench and sat down while grasping its back as though she might fall if she let go.

Jonah watched Rainey from a distance and waited until her panic subsided. He knew Rainey was shocked to see him yesterday. He wanted to give her more time to think about what he had said, but time was critical. Lives could be lost if he hesitated and didn't at least try to enlist her help. He'd made serious mistakes in Arizona and the guilt he carried from SK's escape weighed heavily. How could he convince Rainey to trust him after all that had happened?

A shadow blocked the sunlight and Rainey looked up to see the captain standing in front of her. Before she could react, Jonah sat beside her, clamped a hand on her wrist and while holding it firmly to his side said in a low and urgent voice, "Rainey you have got to listen to me. If you don't, I know you will regret it."

Rainey tried to pull away from Jonah as her eyes looked frantically about to see if anyone was around she could call out to for help. Seeing no one she became very still. She looked Jonah square in the eyes and spat in his face. Jonah didn't move a muscle. He sat there and waited for the scene to play itself out.

"This is still the US of A and I don't have to listen to you. You have nothing to say that interests me. As to unpleasant," Rainey paused, "just the sight of you makes me want to vomit."

Jonah took out a handkerchief and wiped his face. Rainey watched him, her face impassive. "I know you hold me responsible for Sara's death because I withheld information I had about SK until forced to turn it over. I told you I was wrong and I was sorry. I meant it then and I mean it today."

Rainey didn't respond so Jonah tried again. "Rainey, come to Los Angeles and help me with the investigation and capture of SK. You know she intends to kill five more Muslim women and anyone else that gets in her way. You know her better than anyone. She thinks there is a 'relationship' between the two of you, and most importantly, you are the only one to have seen her face. I know that your sketch has been sent across the country to all levels of law enforcement, but Rainey, only you have seen her walk, run, and speak. You know the shape of her head and her body language. If anyone can spot her, you can."

Something in the captain's voice and what he said clicked, and Rainey's chaotic thoughts switched gears. "You said, '...help me with the investigation and capture of SK.' You didn't mention DC Britt and the FBI and you didn't mention any task force in Los Angeles. What haven't you told me, captain?"

Jonah sighed and said abruptly, "Let's walk." He stood and waited for her. Rainey hesitated a few seconds then stood up and joined him as he headed down one of the paths that wound through the park.

They walked for about a quarter of a mile before Jonah spoke again. "First thing I need to clear up. You can call me Jonah. I retired nearly four months ago when I finished rehab for my left arm and shoulder. I'm at about 85% but will never be 100% recovered."

A part of Rainey wanted to say something, maybe a comforting word, but that thought was fleeting. *He got what he deserved*, she thought coldly.

"I'm here on my own. I'm not representing the military, our government, and I'm not in touch with your old boss, DC Britt. I still have some friends in law enforcement circles and I learned he was trying to contact you about consulting and working with the LAPD Task Force."

"SK has surfaced in the LA area?" Rainey asked. Her curiosity and need to know overcame her aversion to Jonah.

"As far as the LAPD is concerned they think they have a copy-cat serial killer and not SK."

"Then why would you or DC Britt think their serial killer is SK?"

"My source tells me DC also thinks it's a copycat because some of the methods used and the choice of victims don't add up. LAPD asked the Bureau for help, so an agent assigned to the LA area is representing the FBI on the task force. I can get into details later if you agree to work with me."

Rainey began to protest, but Jonah stopped walking, paused and said, "I need to answer a more important question for you, Rainey. Why do I think SK is active and on the hunt in LA? Isn't that what you really want to know?"

Rainey nodded and they resumed walking. "After my discharge I couldn't stop thinking about what went down in Arizona. I saved money most of the years I was in the military. Once I retired I bought some of the best computer equipment money can buy and I began to track serial killers operating in the USA. I also tracked shootings where Black Talon ammo surfaced in the commission of any crime."

"But if what you say is true, you're a civilian now and wouldn't have access to the more sensitive information." Rainey's voice trailed off. The captain, or Jonah, being who he was, would not necessarily seek permission for access. "Don't even go there. I don't want to know anything about that," Rainey said sharply.

Jonah looked sideways at Rainey, and seeing storm clouds rising by the look on her face, he controlled the slight smile that had begun to form.

Jonah continued, "The reason I think SK has surfaced is I identified a murder in San Diego about five months ago. The victim was a plastic surgeon who specialized in facial reconstruction. The Vic was shot twice—once in the heart and once in the head with a .22 semi-auto. The bullet fragments recovered from the autopsy were Black Talons. His home was set on fire, but the fire department arrived and the Vic was only partially burned. This is too much of a coincidence for me to ignore."

"SK would have had to get her face changed if she intended to operate as she does out in the open."

"Right," Jonah responded. Rainey and Jonah continued walking. Neither one talked for a few minutes as they were lost in their own thoughts.

"When are you leaving for Los Angeles?"

"When I convince you to agree to go to LA and work with me," Jonah replied.

The idea of tracking down SK without being under DC Britt's thumb and beck and call and not having to deal with inter-agency politics appealed to Rainey. Knowing what they did about SK, Rainey and Jonah just might have a shot at zeroing in on her. Law enforcement could take over afterwards, but finding her might be best served by Jonah's independent methods. Rainey made up her mind.

Rainey fixed her eyes on Jonah's face and he looked back at her grim face. "If I agree to help, understand me, Jonah. I won't be ordered around and I won't be lied to. You won't withhold any information. I am not going to be kept in the dark. Is that clear?"

Jonah nodded and said, "Yes, your terms are clear and I agree."

"I can't leave for at least two days. I have arrangements I need to make about my students' final grades being posted. I'm scheduled to leave in two weeks on a three month archeological expedition in Peru. I've already transferred my office phone to a service and I will need to do this for my home phone. Anyone looking for me in the next week or so will think I am visiting friends and then going out of country on my planned expedition."

"I can wait for you to get done," Jonah said. A tight knot in his chest began to unwind. He could not believe Rainey was going to help, but she said she would and Rainey was a very principled woman, unlike himself, he thought. He did whatever was necessary and broke the rules if he had to. Right now he wasn't going to argue or put any kind of pressure on her.

Rainey answered, "I think you can leave anytime. I will catch a flight out to LA in two days. I also want to touch base with my Muslim contacts in Arizona. They can get me information we'll need about the Muslim communities in LA. I know they can set up some contacts. I want to get hired as a consultant for a Muslim community before I arrive in LA. I don't want to be pressured by DC Britt or any other law enforcement agency and that won't happen if for some reason they have to know I am on a consulting retainer with at least one Muslim community. I can cite conflict of interest to keep them off my back."

"Agreed." Jonah pulled out a business card from his wallet and handed it to Rainey. "When you know your flight and arrival time, give me a call if you need me to pick you up at the airport. Otherwise I'll go ahead and get myself settled in and wait for your call."

Rainey turned the business card over in her hands. It reminded her of the time he had handed her a business card in that restaurant. Sara had been sitting at a table across the dining room and was watching her and Jonah. It was the first time he contacted Rainey. *Sara. How I miss you my dear friend. I'm going to LA for you, Sara. Do you hear me? And I'm going for the five Muslim women that SK is already stalking and planning to kill. This time I'll get her, Sara.*

Rainey and Jonah had walked in a complete circle and were back at the bench Rainey had been sitting on when Jonah approached her earlier. "I've put together information on the copycat serial killer in LA. I'll have Drew drop the file by your place tomorrow."

"Drew?" Rainey raised an eyebrow and took a look at Jonah's new business card. She read *Echo* and a 1-800 phone number. No names and no address. Typical Jonah.

"Drew Holland is one of my field operatives and a partner in Echo. There are three including myself. Guys I've worked with and trust and who are good at what they do. Each of us is an expert in our own field and we are dedicated to the cases Echo takes on. Rand Brown is my other partner. He generally keeps to the East Coast. His sister and parents live on the East Coast and he likes to stay close to them. I don't send him out for field work except for emergencies. You'll probably get to know Rand by phone. Drew, you'll probably see a lot of in LA."

Rainey, for once, didn't know what to say or ask, so she said nothing. She nodded at Jonah and headed out of the park toward home. She'd think of questions to ask him when they met up in LA.

Zarinah
Wednesday

Rainey hurried into her apartment kicking off her shoes on her way to the desk where she tossed her keys and cell phone, grabbed the land-line phone and dialed a number she had memorized many years ago.

"As Salaam' Alaykum."

"Salaams Zarinah. It's me, Rainey. How are you?"

"I haven't changed much since we talked a couple days ago. You didn't call me to ask me how I am, Rainey. I had hoped you would be out of country by now on your way to the excavation site in Peru. You've seen it on the news or read about it, haven't you?" Zarinah was worried and cut right to the chase.

"No, actually I have been so busy with finals, packing, and getting ready to leave for the summer that I haven't read anything or been watching the news." Rainey paused. "You're talking about the Copy Cat killer in Los Angeles and the references to the Scarf Killer, right?"

"So how do you know about this?" Zarinah demanded. "Did that old boss of yours contact you? He better not even think about that. You got out alive, just barely, and you lost too much to get involved in any more serial killer cases, Rainey."

"Well you're not gonna like hearing this but the 'captain' contacted me and…"

"That fool!" Zarinah interrupted loudly. Rainey held the receiver away from her ear. Zarinah had only contempt for Jonah, and while Rainey sympathized, she didn't want to get into that with her right now. She needed Zarinah's help and it was not going to be easy convincing her.

"Listen to me, Zarinah. I don't have a lot of time and I need your help and the help of the Muslim community out in California. I am going to work with the captain regardless. I'd just rather have you at my back and smoothing the way for me. If you don't want to get involved I understand, but I just can't let this go. I've spent a year trying to do just that and it hasn't worked. I'm tired of living with the guilt and feeling of failure. I have to find SK and stop her."

There was a long silence between Rainey and Zarinah as they both calmed down from their high emotions. Each lost in her own thoughts. Finally Zarinah sighed. "This serial killer is supposed to be a copycat, not SK, Rainey. The LA Times reported that the Post-it notes are different and the victims aren't even Muslim women. How can going to California and getting involved in that investigation help you find SK?"

"I'm not going to California to work with the LAPD on that investigation. The captain, now retired, came to see me and brought me information that proves to me that SK is in California and is probably stalking her next victims right now. I am coming to Arizona first and will explain everything in detail once I arrive day after tomorrow. What I need for you to do between now and then is arrange for the Muslim community in Tempe to contract my consulting services. I am hoping you can get Debora to write up a contract and I'll sign it when I see you in Arizona. I also need you to go to the storage shed and get the metal box—you know which one—for me. I need some things from it to take with me to California. Finally, I need for you to find me a safe location in California to stay temporarily. I'd prefer it be within the Muslim community—maybe in the city of Brantlie? I'll explain this later, too. Can you do this, Zarinah?"

"Yes I can do all that, but I don't want to, Rainey. I want you to go on your dig this summer and leave finding SK to the cops. I can't talk you out of this?"

"No, Zarinah. I'm going to California and I am going to work with the captain whether you help or not. It's up to you and the community if I get the Muslims to help. If not, I still need to stop in Arizona to get the metal box and will call you when I arrive. We can have lunch and a short visit before I head for California."

"It's been almost a year and a half since our community lost the first sister. The killings of all three sisters in our communities and the killer still out there free has left open wounds of sorrow and anger. Three of the families on SK's list left the country. The others left the communities. Sis Amel, his intended sixth victim and her family are still in hiding. The community doesn't hold you responsible for SK getting away, Rainey. We all share in your sorrow at losing your best friend and the loss of your grandmother's home. I just don't know if asking the community to get involved again will make things worse."

"I understand, Zarinah, but will you ask for me? Their help might save the lives of other Muslim women in California. We have to try, Zarinah. The LAPD is not interested in the SK case. They are convinced they are investigating a copycat serial killer. The captain is retired and doesn't have access to evidence or reports to anything the police might have that could point to SK. He's working now as a private investigator. He has his own company and is working this SK investigation in California on his own dime."

Rainey waited again for Zarinah to respond. She heard Zarinah faintly speaking in Arabic. She was certain Zarinah was saying *dua*, which is a prayer asking for God's help.

"I'll talk to the imams and Deb and will let you know once you arrive in Phoenix. I can't promise anything, Rainey, but I will do my best to convince them. I'll ask the imam to contact the imam in Brantlie. What I don't want is the community in Brantlie to panic. Especially because you are telling me the cops aren't looking for SK in connection with the Copy Cat killer."

"Thanks and a big hug. I know that none of the Muslim families fitting the profile of SK will really feel safe again until we catch SK. I won't feel safe and I'm not a Muslim. See you at the airport. I'll call back when I have my flight number and arrival time. Salaams, Zarinah".

"Wa alaykum as salaam, Rainey."

Zarinah's husband Habibullah remained quiet while he listened to his wife's end of the conversation. He could see how troubled she was, but he agreed with Rainey. "I don't think it will take much to convince the imams to sign a contract for consulting services with Rainey. They don't have the same feelings you have for her, dear. They will want to do whatever they can to help find that killer. I know Sister Deb will hesitate like you are doing, but it's better we help Rainey than let her go out there with that captain guy on her own. You know that."

Zarinah looked up at her husband and gave him a rueful smile. "Ol' man, you don't have to tell me what I already know."

Bibi patted his wife's arm. "You don't have much time. I'll call the brothers and we can go to the storage shed after we meet with them. You call Deb now so she can get the contract written and faxed to the imam in Tempe."

Rainey worked well past midnight to finish grading her students' final exams and prepared the final grade list for her assistant professor, Carlye Wright. She would post the grades and field the students' questions and complaints. Rainey hoped she would have no trouble falling asleep that night, but her thoughts kept coming back to Jonah's plan and her role in it. Long into the early morning hours Rainey thought and planned. Around four AM she finally drifted off into a restless sleep.

Drew
Thursday

At nine AM East Coast time, six AM Arizona time, Rainey called Zarinah and filled her in on what additional help she needed and what Rainey planned to be doing in California with Jonah's Echo PIs hunting SK. She was elated to learn that the imams in three communities had signed a contract for her consulting services and the metal box was waiting for her. Now if Zarinah could pull together the rest of what Rainey needed by the time she got to Arizona tomorrow, Rainey felt confident her plan had a chance.

At seven o'clock she was busy on the phone making travel arrangements and contacting Professor Raymond Lehman, who was heading up the archeological expedition in Peru in two weeks. Raymond was not happy to learn that Rainey might be joining the expedition late. How late, Rainey was not able to say.

After a light breakfast of a cream cheese bagel and green tea, Rainey dressed in her jogging shorts, a tank top, and running shoes. She was looking forward to working off some of her stress since she had talked with Jonah yesterday.

The intercom buzzer sounded just as Rainey put her hand on her front door. With a sigh of exasperation Rainey back tracked and pressed the intercom next to her desk. "Ms. Walker, George from Security, here."

"Good morning, George."

"I have a gentleman in the lobby says he's from Echo. A Mr. Drew Hollahand is requesting to visit you. I verified his ID and he checks out. Do I send him on up or do you want to come down? He says he has some files he needs to deliver."

"Wait five minutes and then send him on up, and thanks, George."

"No problem, Ms. Walker."

The extra fee I pay each month for security and screening is worth every penny, Rainey thought as she changed from her running outfit to a pair of casual slacks, flats, and a white blouse. Her friends had a personal pass code they gave to security. Anyone else was screened and Rainey contacted first before they could use the elevators to reach her loft apartment. The security screening was a precaution Rainey had felt necessary as the Scarf Killer was still 'out there' and had tried to kill her a year ago in Arizona.

Rainey opened the door when the buzzer sounded. Drew Hollahand filled the open doorway at 6' 5" and 280 pounds of raw muscle. He was an imposing figure. His dark brown hair was cut in a 1950's crew cut and his rugged face was marred by a jagged scar running from his right temple across his face ending at the left side of his face about an inch beyond his lower lip. He was wearing tan Docker slacks, a tan button-down shirt, a tan sports coat and tan loafers, at least a size 17. He held out a soft briefcase that looked almost like a miniature in his beefy hands. Rainey felt over-whelmed until he spoke in the softest voice that seemed incongruous in such a huge man.

"Ms. Walker, Jonah said to drop off these files and answer any questions you might have about them. May I come in?"

Rainey felt her cheeks burn when she realized she had been openly staring at this soft-spoken giant. "I apologize for just standing here. Do come in Mr. Hollahand."

"Drew."

"Drew," Rainey repeated as she stepped to the side so he could enter her apartment. "I'm Rainey. If we are going to work together let's get on first name basis."

Drew nodded as he walked into the living area of the loft and slowly did a visual before sitting down on the couch. Drew cleared his throat and said, "Nice place."

"Thanks. Can I offer you something to drink? Water, iced tea? A soda?"

"Nothing for me, I'm good."

Rainey took the chair across the coffee table from Drew and put the briefcase on top of the table between them.

Drew glanced at the paper to the left of the briefcase and Rainey followed his eyes as he seemed to be reading the document. "That's my airline ticket to Phoenix. I'll be stopping there first before I head to California. I'll be renting a vehicle in Arizona and driving."

Drew nodded and waited for Rainey to speak again.

Not much of a conversationalist, Rainey thought. "I'll read the file on my flight to Arizona. Why don't you give me a brief summary of the file contents and any ideas or thoughts you might have."

Drew looked closely at Rainey and it appeared he was struggling with what he was going to say. "I wrote a summary for you about the Copy Cat file. You can read it later. Both Jonah and I think the Copy Cat killer is linked to SK, but we don't have anything concrete to take to the LAPD task force. Jonah thinks using you as bait will cause SK to surface—show her hand. I think it's a bad idea, but he's usually right about these things."

Rainey was surprised at his candor and said so.

"I work with, and not for Jonah. We are partners and I'm not a yes man. Neither is Rand, our other partner, but in serious stuff where we don't agree, Rand and I generally go with Jonah's judgment."

"I see," Rainey replied, but she really didn't see. Rainey just didn't know what to say at this point. Maybe when I get to know

Drew and Rand better I'll understand the Echo partnership? The partners disagreeing…this is perfect. I may have a member of the team supporting my idea and he can be the messenger…break the news to Jonah, Rainy thought before she broached her plan to Drew.

"I agree with you, Drew. Going to California as Rainey Walker, former FBI agent is not in my best interests. I don't cotton to being exposed as a sitting duck for SK. It would hamper my ability to move around in Muslim communities and make me an easier target for SK. I don't relish being a sitting duck for SK. She's smart and I am not relying on Jonah, his team, or any law enforcement team to protect me."

"I see your point. So why are you going to LA?" Drew asked. The puzzlement showing on his face was the bait Rainey was looking for to reel him in.

"When I arrive in California I will be traveling with my aunt and uncle. I will be presented to the Muslim community in Brantlie as an Iraqi refugee. Brantlie is a college city and also the hub of a large Muslim community. My cover will be that I am there to spend the summer working at the Sultana Bookstore & More department store earning money and getting prepared for university in the fall. I will be covered with hijab scarf, veil, and gloves. I will join the various sister groups at the local mosque. Using this cover I will learn a lot more that way, and if SK surfaces in a Muslim woman's disguise I'll be waiting for her. She may already be in this community, so my friends in Arizona will be contacting the leaders in this community to identify potential Muslim women meeting SK's victim profile. My undercover persona will fit it perfectly."

A slow grin spread across Drew's face. *Jonah has met his match with this smart and devious woman.* Rainey's plan looked good on paper but there were flaws. "I see a few holes in this plan of yours. If I may point them out?"

Rainey had anticipated Drew would try and discourage her. Something she knew Jonah would do just because it wasn't his plan. What he said next surprised her. His comments were not in that line of thinking. His comments were more like examining a strategic plan and looking for weaknesses.

"You are not a Muslim, and even though you grew up with a Muslim grandmother in a Muslim community and have Muslim friends, you haven't practiced the prayer rituals and such. You don't speak Arabic and this could present an even greater obstacle. SK speaks Arabic and has learned Muslim etiquette and Arab culture, so she would fit into the Muslim communities."

"Good points, Drew, but I spent the last year learning how to read and write Arabic. My instructor was an Iraqi emigrant. I have practiced Arabic speaking with my Muslim friends at the university. I have been to several different mosques on many occasions. I do know how to prepare for the prayer and how to pray. While in Arizona I dug out my grandmother's Islam 101 book, which was a primer for learning the basics about practicing Islam and learning about Islam's historical places and persons. A year ago, my good friend Zarinah ran interference for me, but I was at a big disadvantage when it came to talking with community members and gaining their trust. So since then, I've been preparing for the day when SK surfaced again. I wanted to be ready and have this ability to help when the time came."

"Why are you going to Brantlie and not LA? I don't understand this strategy."

"A copycat killer is operating in LA and is getting a lot of press. No way would SK be upstaged by someone else. Brantlie has one of the largest concentrations of multi ethnic Muslims in California. The community is large, but not overly large like LA where the Muslim population is spread out in many suburbs. SK will look for a community similar to those in Arizona that have potential victim targets meeting her criteria. If she doesn't have a target in Brantlie already, she will when I arrive, and she will know about my arrival. She has always tracked the community activity where she intends to stalk."

"I wasn't expecting you to be this prepared. Jonah said you were really reluctant to join him or even a task force and had been avoiding contact with your prior employer, the FBI."

"That's true. I am still reluctant. I still feel fear just thinking about that destructive and psychotic killer. I won't work as a law enforcement officer again or be a part of a multi-jurisdictional task force. What Jonah offered, though, gives me some control and will allow me to use my judgment and skills. That's why I changed my mind."

"Jonah is going to be really ticked off with your change in his plans, Rainey. I'm glad I won't be around when the fireworks begin!" Drew gave Rainey a rueful smile while shaking his head.

"Oh, but you are going to be around when Jonah learns his plans have been changed. In fact, you are the one who is going to tell him, and not until after I leave on my flight to Arizona tomorrow morning." Rainey's eyes twinkled when she saw the dumb-struck look on Drew's face. Slowly her smile widened and she started to laugh. Drew looked at her fiercely for a moment and then he too began to laugh. Rainey had won him over.

"Okay. I'll wait and break the news. He's driving the command van out to LA. I'll just wait until he calls me after he arrives and give him your plan of action. Maybe I'll tape it for ya."

"No need. I'm sure as soon as he hangs up on you, I'll be getting messages on my cell. I won't be answering until my new relatives and I cross the Arizona - California state line."

Drew stood and offered Rainy his huge paw to shake. Rainey shook it and walked him to the door. Drew turned as he entered the hallway and said, "I can't wait to call Rand. He is gonna love this!"

"Tell Rand I look forward to meeting or talking with him soon, and thanks, Drew."

Drew nodded and was in the elevator and gone before Rainey shut and locked her door.

Copy Cat Murders
Friday

Rainey booked a first class seat so she would have plenty of room to read the file in relative privacy without someone looking over at the pages. She set aside Drew's summary and read the file beginning to end in order to form some initial impressions. After reading through the file a second time, she had to agree with the LAPD task force. There were just too many inconsistencies in the Copy Cat killer's methods and choice of victims. What seemed obvious was that there had to have been a leak about the Post-it note placed on the Phoenix cop that SK had murdered labeling him "collateral damage- 0". The three copycat victims were labeled with Post-it notes left on their bodies with the words "collateral damage" with a number. Most significant to Rainey was the Copy Cat's choice of female victims; none were Muslim and none had their faces mutilated. Why the killer placed a headscarf over their faces was something only the killer could explain.

Rainy set aside the file and began reading the summary notes Drew had prepared for her. Maybe somewhere in them he connected the Copy Cat killer to SK. So far, the only convincing or credible information Jonah had provided pointing to SK surfacing in California was the killing of the plastic surgeon in San Diego. The killer's method of using a .22 caliber revolver and

Black Talon ammo, and setting the doctor's home on fire was a carbon copy kill profile of the murdered plastic surgeon SK had killed in Mexico. The problem, Rainey thought, was that there was nothing in the Copy Cat report file that linked the San Diego killing to the LA serial killings.

Rainey finished the summary and rubbed her eyes. She leaned back in her seat, closed her eyes and thought about what Drew had written. The link was tenuous. It could simply be just more of the Copy Cat operating under SK's methodology. Law enforcement estimates there are a couple dozen or more "unsub" or unidentified serial killers operating in the USA today. Some may never be identified. Many are discovered only through some unrelated incident and not because law enforcement is actively tracking or looking for these psychotic killers. It would not be a stretch to believe that two different serial killers were active at the same time in California, but Rainey did not believe that SK would share media attention in LA with another serial killer.

Victim 1 had been paralyzed in the same manner as the Phoenix cop and then was stabbed multiple times in the chest causing death from the literal shredding of her heart by the killer. Victim 2 was poisoned with cyanide ingested from eating a chocolate brownie. Victim 3 was shot in the heart, but Black Talon ammo was not used. The Black Talon ammo was a closely guarded fact held back by Phoenix police and had not leaked to the media. All three victims were killed in their homes without forced entry. The cops believed the victims knew the killer or had some reason to trust the killer enough to let the killer into their homes. *Some coincidences or contrivance by the Copy Cat killer?* Rainey wondered.

The only forensic evidence found at two of the crime scenes were strands of human hair that were not the victims, but determined to be hair used in a natural human hair wig. The strands of hair left at both scenes came from the same wig. *Was this carelessness or intentional on the part of the killer?*

The last paragraph contained the conclusions of the Echo PIs and the idea was one Rainey had not considered.

"There is a possibility that during the year SK has been under the radar, she met the Copy Cat killer and they are working together, or at the least know each other."

Pretty thin and nothing I read leads me to this conclusion, Rainey thought. The plastic surgeon's murder in San Diego points strongly to SK being active in California. Most probably stalking and planning her kills at this point. The Copy Cat killings may be a bonus to SK. Everyone's attention is on LA and the Copy Cat killings. No one is connecting the San Diego killing to the one in Mexico and linking both to SK's murders in Arizona, for that matter.

Rainey wasn't sorry she decided to work with Jonah and Echo. She believed that SK was going to begin killing again, and soon. This time Rainey was determined to put an end to the killing and to SK.

Copy Cat
Friday night

His palms were sweating and his breathing quickened. He had finally made contact with SK again, and persuaded her to meet with him. He was too arrogant and vain to admit to himself that it was actually SK who had found him. She had agreed to meet him once, but had been a no show. Then the second message came, and a new meeting was set up for tomorrow. He hoped that she left him another message while he was out tonight.

Christopher brought his thoughts back to the woman sitting across the table. He briefly kissed her hand and told her he would be calling her soon. He apologized for being inattentive most of the evening and explained to the stupid woman calling herself by the ridiculous name of Dee-Dee that he had been preoccupied by a business deal he was about to close. Dee-Dee was quick to accept any excuse he handed her.

This was their second dinner date. He had suggested caution because of the horrible killings in the news, so they met at an up-scale restaurant rather than her hotel suite. All evening Dee-Dee had been tossing out blatant hints that he was welcome to go back to the Waldorf Hotel suite with her once dinner ended.

Dee-Dee was getting a free pass tonight. He was in a hurry to get home to check the group message board. Dee-Dee could live and dream another night about her dark haired, blue-eyed, muscular Adonis.

Christopher called a taxi and walked Dee-Dee to the curb. As they waited for the taxi he gently kissed her on the lips, snickering inwardly at the way the idiot all but swooned. Watching the taxi pull away with Dee-Dee safe inside, he suddenly felt uneasy, as if someone was watching him. He looked around. There it was again. That creepy feeling he'd had earlier in the evening that left him feeling cold. Christopher's eyes quickly scanned both sides of the street and he looked at the empty parked cars. Nothing. He unconsciously shook his head and then stepped up to the curbing and whistled for a taxi.

Christopher gave the cabbie directions and sat back in the seat and thought about the evening. He should have taken care of Dee-Dee tonight. That was his plan, but something didn't feel right. He'd felt all evening as if someone was watching him. He had brought the briefcase with him and told her he had rushed straight from the office and hadn't even stopped at home to freshen up. The silly woman had just simpered thinking he could barely stand to be apart from her. All during dinner he kept thinking about SK and hoping there would be a message left for him on the message board, but first he had to stop at the apartment.

SK

Friday night

I can't believe I have to do the LAPD task force's job for them, she mumbled, while watching as the man stepped up to the curbing and whistled for a taxi. SK yawned and gathered up her equipment and thermos. She checked the roof for any evidence she might have left and finding none, headed for the door to the stairway leading down to the top floor of the apartment building.

SK took the stairs to the ground level and walked though the deserted underground parking lot. The apartment building was under construction and the only one around at night was night security and he was sound asleep in what would become the manager's office.

SK wasn't in any hurry to follow the Copy Cat. She knew where he lived and would soon be investigating his apartment. She had already been inside Jimmy-boy's penthouse apartment, spending an hour setting up micro surveillance cameras so she could track what he did when he was home behind closed doors. *Who was doing the killing? Copy Cat or Jimmy-boy? Were they doing them together? No matter. All the murders had been done by an inept killer. If I can find out information about Copy Cat and Jimmy-boy, what does this say about the skill of the LAPD task force? The cops don't have a single lead as to who the Copy Cat killer is or what is the motivation for the killings. The LAPD is even less than incompetent,* she thought.

SK walked to her SUV parked behind a club four blocks from the surveillance site. She'd paid the valet a hefty tip to park close to the fire door behind the club. SK removed her black jump suit, running shoes, and stored her equipment in the back end of the SUV. She put the .22 with silencer in her handbag while slipping her feet into three inch heels and fastened the gold straps. She locked the SUV and using a key, opened the back exit door and went inside the club.

SK walked through the crowded room to the bar and ordered a martini with a double olive, drank it slowly, and then signaled to the bar tender that she was ready to pay her tab. Her target should be home by now if he had not made any stops. She walked to the door and smiled at the doorman and the valet who rushed to get her vehicle. SK considered the valet. By his size and the intelligence she saw in his eyes, she wondered why he'd settle for a dead-end job when any branch of the military would prepare him for a great career after serving his country.

Maybe he doesn't want to get shot up or blown to pieces by some terrorist, the hideous grating voice in her head mocked her. The smile on SK's face transformed into a fierce scowl as she said through gritted teeth, "Stop it. Not now. Leave me alone!"

The doorman touched SK lightly on her arm and asked, "Are you okay, Miss?"

SK quickly recovered. "I'm fine. I'm just ticked off at the run I found in my nylons. Thanks for your concern."

The doorman nodded and went back inside the club. *Nosey scumbag. Where the hell is that valet?* SK heard where the valet and her SUV were. The sound of squealing tires and crunching metal had SK slipping out of her shoes, grabbing them and double-timing it down the alley to the back parking lot. She rounded the corner of the building to see her SUV and a Cadillac Seville facing each other with the front ends mashed. The Caddy got the worst of it. The valet was climbing out of the SUV while the driver of the Caddy had her face mashed into the front airbag.

Intelligent? The voice in her head mocked her as she turned sideways, opened her purse and extracted the .22 from it and attached the silencer. "You okay?" She asked approaching the dazed valet with a concerned look on her face. "Is my SUV drivable?"

The valet stammered, "I'm sorry. The caddy came out of nowhere and I…"

The voice purred softly, *Easy now. Don't let him see your anger. Steady. You gotta get out of here before the cops arrive. Find out about the SUV. The Caddy driver's still knocked out. Just moaning. You can take care of that pain for her in a minute.* "Is my SUV drivable?"

"Yes. I backed it up some and it seems okay. Just a small dent in the …" *Pop, Pop.* The valet's eyes rolled up as two small red dots appeared and began spreading in the center of mass in his chest. He pitched forward, hitting the pavement without finishing his sentence. SK walked over to the driver's door of the Caddy and put two shots in the groaning girl's head. She swept the interior of the caddy with her eyes and saw that the driver was alone.

SK hurried to the opened driver's door to her SUV. The engine was still running. She backed up straight a hundred feet and turned the wheel backing into an empty parking space. She then put the vehicle in drive, pulled forward, and drove out of the parking lot, heading south to avoid the club's front entrance. SK did not hear any sirens, but it was only a matter of time before that doorman noticed the valet was missing.

The white noise began deep inside her head as a low buzz and the pain started. *Not now! Not now!* SK moaned. *Think. Think. I have to ditch this SUV and get some new wheels. I can't be driving it very far.*

No shit, shineola, the voice in her head mocked her. *The damage is noticeable and the paint transfer will tell the cops the color of vehicle, and the height of the transfer will indicate that the missing accident vehicle is a truck or SUV. Unless the responding cop is a bozo, you'd better pull over and just leave the SUV now.*

"I can't," SK argued with the voice in her head. "I can't leave the equipment. I don't have time to sanitize it."

Burn it, Stupid! the voice shouted to be heard over the white noise now pounding inside SK's head.

SK remembered a used car dealership about a quarter mile north on Edgeworth Drive up ahead to her right. She made the turn onto Edgeworth and made a left turn into the alleyway and stopped the SUV behind the dealership. The lighting was almost non-existent. SK's luck was holding as the street lights had been taken out by vandals. The shattered glass littered the ground.

SK climbed into the rear of the SUV and quickly changed into her jumpsuit and pulled on her running shoes. She used her keys to open the locked utility box and pulled out a length of rubber hose while grabbing a book of matches. Tossing the wig in a back-pack with the night vision glasses, spare ammo and .45, she made a quick inspection of the utility box and SUV interior, making sure that nothing that might survive the fire could be traced back to her. The registration and plates belonged to a deceased woman who had the misfortune to have accepted a lunch invitation from SK.

SK grabbed the slim-jim and headed for the car lot. The lock on the back gate was a joke and took her three seconds to open. She scanned the lot looking for an SUV to boost and found a dark blue one with a rear side window cracked. A few minutes later the new SUV was hot-wired and SK drove it through the gate. She parked it five hundred feet away and walked back to the damaged SUV. She opened the lock to the gas tank and used the rubber hose to siphon gas from the tank through the rubber hose and into the SUV. The rubber hose was just long enough to fit inside the SUV and she kept it in place by the rolled up window. In just minutes the floor of the SUV was flooded with gasoline. SK struck a match and put it to the book of matches. As the matches flared, SK tossed the matches into the SUV and sprinted to her new ride without looking back when the SUV began burning and then exploded. SK was fascinated by fire but had no time to enjoy this one.

SK grinned. The white noise crawled back into its hole and the voice had nothing to ridicule her about. She had made a clean get away. SK looked at the face of her watch. It was two AM. She was tired. SK decided to call it a day. Copy Cat didn't know it but he had been given a short reprieve.

Arizona
Friday noon

The hot Arizona sun caused Rainey to break out in a sweat, as she placed the metal box and her luggage in the trunk of the rental car Zarinah had already rented for her. She closed the trunk and turned to give Zarinah a hug. "I can't thank you enough, Zarinah. The paperwork is just what I needed. I'll be sure to call you after I meet with the imams in Yuma later this afternoon."

"You just watch your back, Rainey. The brothers will have all the information you need to join the community in Brantlie. Meeting in Yuma was their smart idea. This way no one in the community will know anything to accidentally tell anyone else about you being there and your investigation. Deb said she wants to hear from you soon. She's as worried as I am about you getting involved again."

"I am not going to do anything other than try to identify SK if she is masquerading as a sister."

"Sure, and I am sitting in this wheel chair because I took a notion I didn't feel like walking today," Zarinah tossed back at Rainey.

Rainey grinned at Zarinah and her droll humor.

"I don't think there is a sister left in California that meets those requirements that psycho uses to pick her victims, that is, except for you posing as a sister."

"I hope this doesn't spook SK," Rainey answered. Rainey's concern was for the safety of the intended women victims as well as others. SK had shown she was unpredictable when her plans were thwarted.

"As soon as we got the word out last year, most of the families with potential victims moved almost immediately. California is just too close to Arizona for comfort. There are two sisters and their families left in the Brantlie community and they are ready to leave as soon as you get there. And nobody is talking. Nobody!"

"I am not doubting the silence of the Muslims in the communities, but I know how hard it is to keep something this huge hidden," Rainey said.

"After what happened here in Arizona with the killer getting away, there was a regional meeting of all the masjid leaders. A door to door canvas of all Muslim homes was done to identify any families fitting that killer's victim profile. Funds were gathered and set aside to relocate the families. Like here in Arizona, some families returned to the husband's native homeland while other families moved to other states and into new communities. National origin is not entered into masjid membership listings now, so the killer can't easily find Iraqi families."

"And no one in law enforcement is aware of these steps taken by the California Muslim communities?"

"Not as far as I know," Zarinah replied.

Rainey shook her head trying to figure out how this had escaped the attention of law enforcement. The potential victims moving out of California would make it harder for SK to find victims and was an effective way of slowing down the killer. It would also make setting a trap almost impossible with no victims for SK to stalk.

"After what you went through, I just didn't want to talk about anything that happened last year unless you brought up the subject. If the LA cops don't think the Copy Cat killer is SK, then they won't be interested in listening to what the Muslims have to say anyways," Zarinah flatly stated.

"You are probably right."

Rainey looked at her wristwatch to check the time. "I've got to get a move on if I am going to get to Yuma in time for that meeting. Love you so much, and I will stay in touch." Rainey bent down and hugged Zarinah, noticing a few tears rolling down her face.

Zarinah sniffed into her sleeve and then smiled at Rainey. "Allah be with you, Rainey Walker. Salaams."

"Salaams and God be with you, too," Rainey said and got into the rental car before she too started to cry.

Yuma Meeting
Friday afternoon

Rainey arrived at the Sundown Restaurant just a few minutes late. She hurried to lock the car and get out of the late afternoon heat. The restaurant's AC blew a cool blast of air on her face when she opened the door. Taking a quick visual of the large dining room and lunch counter Rainey spotted the group of Muslims, five men and two women, seated at a large table in a corner of the dining room. Rainey walked back to the table and stood behind the one empty chair between the two women.

"As Salaam'Alaykum," the seven Muslims greeted her.

"Wa Alaykum as Salaam," Rainey replied and took her seat at the table. A waitress approached Rainey and she ordered black coffee and a large glass of water. The waitress brought the coffee and water and then returned to the lunch counter.

"We thank you for meeting with us. I am called Salim," Salim said and introduced the four men and the two women who were the wives of two of the men.

The people seated at the table nodded at Rainey and then looked back at Salim. *Seems like Salim is going to be the spokesperson for the group*, Rainey thought. She was wrong. Salim passed an envelope to the man to his right and the envelope was passed along until it came to Rainey. Her name was printed on the envelope.

"Inside are the background summaries of your temporary Aunt Jamilah and Uncle Ibrahim you will be staying with in Brantlie. Your uncle owns a group of rental bungalows and one has been reserved for you. He nodded to one of the men at the table and his wife who was sitting next to Rainey.

Rainey smiled at the woman and nodded her head at the woman's husband.

"My wife will introduce you as her niece. We will take you to the Sultana Books & More and introduce you to Brother Khalid who is the owner and who will give you a job in sales. My nephew will loan you his car so you will not need to rent a vehicle. It is a very good car, a newer model and safe for you to use when you need to meet with the investigators working with you."

Rainey thanked her new temporary uncle and then waited to see who else had something to say before she talked to the group.

"In the envelope are the phone numbers of each brother here at the table. If you need anything please call one of us. We chose the name Amira for you and the last name of Brother Ibrahim. Your father is supposed to be his brother. I suggest you leave all personal identification information with Brother Ibrahim for now. You will need to get used to using cash for purchases. Money for this is in the envelope and when you need more just ask Brother Ibrahim."

Another man at the table addressed her as Amira and spoke to her in Arabic. All seven Muslims looked at Rainey to see if she would respond.

Rainey answered in Arabic that she had learned to speak and read in Arabic and that she knew how to perform wudu and the prayer ritual for each of the five prayers.

Rainey breathed a sigh of relief when all of them smiled at her for the first time. She felt as if the ice had finally been broken and the stiffness of the group dissipated.

"Good, Rainey Walker. Learning to speak and read Arabic is not so easy. It will not be so hard for you to pretend to be Amira, niece of Ibrahim," Salim stated, and the other Muslims nodded in agreement.

Rainey took a deep breath. *Now is as good a time as any. I may as well just jump right in and say what I have to say and then see what their response is.* "Zarinah told me about the situation in California...moving the Iraqi families out of the communities. Have you informed the law enforcement officials about this?"

Salim looked at Rainey and said, "No we have not had any contact with California police officials. Last year, an official from the Phoenix police contacted me and a few other imams, but after the killer escaped from Arizona, we have not been contacted since."

"Do you recall the name of the Phoenix police official?"

"His name was Lieutenant Jerald. He said he was the head of their task force. He is the one who informed us that the Arizona case was still open but the police believed the killer had left Arizona. Of course, we already knew this by reading the newspapers and watching the news. We also keep in touch with the imams in Arizona. We always had a concern that the killer could come to California. We did appreciate that Phoenix police officer calling the imams here in California."

Rainey acknowledged what Salim said and then shared some of her plans with those present. "I will be working with a private investigations company while I am in California. Unless the LAPD contacts me and requests my help or there is some indication that their Copy Cat serial killer they are investigating has a connection to the SK, I will not become involved in the Copy Cat investigation in LA. My reason for coming to California and to your community is that I hope I will be able to spot SK if she is hanging around within your communities. I know my role is that of a potential target for this killer, but I was trained as a law enforcement officer and your sisters, wives, and nieces are not. Let us hope that if the killer begins stalking in Brantlie that I am the one she begins to stalk."

"What happens if you do see this killer in our community? Will you call the local police or the FBI and report this?" Salim asked.

"At some point, we will need to talk with the local police. Right now everyone is focused on the Copy Cat killings in LA. It will be difficult to get any focus on SK unless we can provide some concrete evidence that she is operating in California and most probably in Brantlie. They won't be pleased that we have set me up as a potential target for her," Rainey replied.

The men at the table nodded their heads in agreement. Abdullah raised his hand and spoke up, "I work as a manager at one of the hotels in Brantlie. My eldest son Rashid is the publisher of the Brantlie Muslim Voice. It is a weekly newspaper. We thought that we would publish an interview with Brother Ibrahim about the arrival of his niece to the community and provide the information that the niece will be working this summer at the Sultana store while waiting for classes to begin for the Fall semester. The newspaper will be published tomorrow if this is okay with you to do this. If the killer is in our communities pretending to be a sister, then she will read about your arrival. We thought this might be of help to you?"

"That is an excellent idea, Abdullah. Please thank your son for me." Abdullah smiled at the other men at the table, his pride in his son's accomplishments very evident.

Salim looked at his wrist watch. "I think if Rainey has nothing else at this moment, we need to get ready to begin our return trip. Brother Ibrahim and his wife drove to this meeting and you will ride back with them. The rest of us flew here in a small plane and will be returning by plane."

Everyone stood and Salim paid the check. Rainey thanked each of the Muslim men and smiled at the other female, introduced as Salim's wife, Saba. Rainey watched as this larger group left the restaurant.

As Rainey picked up the envelope from the table she turned

to Ibrahim and said, "I completely forgot about the car Zarinah rented for me. I can't leave it parked here."

"Don't be concerned. I am calling a friend who will be here in about fifteen minutes. He will take care of the rental car. We can transfer your luggage to my car and wait for his arrival. It should not be long."

Rainey walked out of the restaurant with Ibrahim and his wife Jamilah. After transferring her things to their car she took a small suitcase and went back inside the restaurant to use the ladies room to put on a *hijab* scarf and *abeya*. She also needed to call Jonah to fill him in on the meeting and what she had learned from the group of Muslims.

Jonah
Friday – LA

Rainey looked in the mirror above the sink and adjusted the head scarf but left the face veil hanging loose. She would cover her face once they were close to Brantlie. She put the gloves in her handbag. It was going to be difficult getting use to wearing these outer clothes in the summer heat. At least it would be ten to fifteen degrees cooler in California than it was in the Arizona desert. Taking out her cell phone, she dialed the number on the Echo business card Jonah had given her.

"Rainey where are you? Did you make it to California or are you still in Arizona? I have been trying to reach you for the last six hours. DC Britt has called me four times hounding me to tell him where you are. He says something urgent has come up and he must talk to you and he's not buying that I don't know where you are."

Rainey heard the frustration in Jonah's voice and decided to step lightly. There was too much to tell him and she did not want to spend a bunch of time on the phone arguing with him. "I'm in Yuma, Arizona and getting ready to travel by car to Brantlie, California with my 'cover' aunt and uncle. I turned off my phone as I came into Yuma, driving from Phoenix earlier and I've been in a meeting for the last hour or so. I don't intend to get into a shouting match with you, Jonah."

"Okay. Okay, but we have got to stay in touch. No more shutting off your phone. Agreed?"

"Agreed. Before I get started, what did DC want to talk to me about? Any ideas?"

"He wouldn't tell me, but I feel certain it has to do with SK. If the LA task force working the Copy Cat investigation wanted to consult with you, I'm sure someone would have left a message with your service, right?"

"I would think so, but maybe they contacted DC because I used to work for the FBI?"

"Possibly, but I just don't get any vibes that the task force is interested in SK. They seem pretty sure the Copy Cat killer is someone else."

"Where'd you get that intel from?"

"If you must know, Bob Jerald and I touch bases now and then."

"Hmmm. At the meeting I had with the Muslim imams from California today, one of the men mentioned it was Lieutenant Jerald who contacted them about the SK investigation in Arizona. They don't seem to have a problem with him like the Arizona communities had."

"He's scheduled to fly back to Arizona tomorrow. I'd like him to meet with us and possibly Drew and Rand before he leaves. He's willing to meet with us. We just need a time and location. He told me he is concerned about the Black Talon ammo showing up in the San Diego killing of that plastic surgeon."

"So I'm going to get to meet the other Echo partner in person?"

"Drew thought his size would be difficult to disguise. Rand is about 5'7 and is African-American. It'll be easier for him to do surveillance and keep tabs on you in the Brantlie community."

Rainey glanced at her wrist watch. "Jonah, I have some people waiting on me and we need to get started to Brantlie. Right now

I need to make a quick call to DC Britt and also check with my message service. I have my notebook. I'll send you an email briefing. I'll get back to you later this evening. This will give you some time to digest the briefing report I'll be sending and find a meet location for tomorrow. Okay with you?"

Rainey waited, hearing only silence from the other end of the phone. She pictured Jonah with a deep furrow in his forehead and frown on his well-defined lips. Jonah wasn't a patient man, but he knew he had no choice but to wait.

"Fine" was his curt reply. The phone line went dead and Rainey grinned at it before using the speed dial to check with her answering service.

Es Que

"Twenty-four seven Madge speaking. How may I help you?" Any incoming calls Janice didn't recognize the phone number for were answered with this line by Janice.

"Hi Janice. It's Rainey. I'm using a throw away cell phone because I left my Blackberry at home. I didn't want to lose it on the expedition." Rainey verified her personal information with Janice and asked for her messages. Rainey had been using the 24/7 messaging service for seven years, and no matter day or night, Janice always answered her calls.

"Good thing you called in. I have two callers leaving urgent messages for you. The first one is a caller you know, your prior boss, DC Britt. He's left half a dozen messages asking you to call him and all are marked urgent. Nothing said about what he needs to speak to you about. The second caller is from an unidentified female. She's left three messages for you using a different name each time, but the voice is the same although she did a pretty good job of trying to disguise her voice."

"That sounds interesting. What did this female caller say?"

"Didn't really make much sense to me. She spelled out the message all three times and said for me to be sure you got the message. I tried to explain that you were out of country on an expedition, but she cut me off all three times."

"Wait a moment Janice, while I get a pencil and notepad."

"Don't think you'll need to because the message is short. Ready?"

"Go ahead, Janice."

"She spelled the letters E and S then paused and then she spelled out the letters Q and U and E. That's all she said." Janice repeated the message a second time for Rainey.

Rainey felt like she'd been sucker punched in the stomach and her breath caught in her throat. *How did she find me? Oh my god*, Rainey gasped for breath. *ES or S and QUE or K... SK*. Rainey made the connection. The silence lengthened between Rainey and Janice.

"Rainey. Rainey? Are you okay? Is something wrong?" Janice asked.

Rainey heard the unfamiliar note of anxiety in Janice's voice. Janice was seldom rattled about anything she heard or was told through the message service.

"I'm fine, Janice. If this woman calls again ask her if she would like to leave a phone number for me, but don't do any chit-chat. Keep it straight forward and say as little as possible, okay?"

"Sure Rainey, no problem. Enjoy your excavation and have some fun. Bye"

"I plan too. Bye, Janice."

Rainey felt sick but didn't have time to think about SK at the moment. She poked her head out of the ladies' restroom door and looked out the large plate-glass window. She saw her temporary aunt and uncle waiting patiently inside the car for her. *I'd better call DC and keep it short. We really need to get on the road.*

DC Britt
Friday – FBI Headquarters

"DC Britt."

"DC, my message service told me you had called several times leaving urgent messages. So what's so urgent that you called me six times? I sent you an email advising I was going on a dig in Peru. Didn't you get my email?"

"Don't try that BS with me Rainey. Your message service told me nothing so I called your professor friend, identified myself as head of the FBI Profilers Division, and after a little arm twisting he told me you weren't leaving with the group. Said you were delayed for a couple of weeks. He assumed it was some law enforcement consulting job with the FBI that needed your immediate attention. Now we know that's not what delayed your joining the expedition, don't we?"

DC's voice dripped with sarcasm. He was pretty steamed up. DC was not used to being ignored.

Rainey counted to five to calm herself. She needed information and not an argument with DC. "Yes, I am still in the States and will be for a few weeks. I have a consulting job that came up at the last minute and felt it necessary to provide my services. I remind you that I am not employed by the FBI anymore and I am not at your beck and call, DC. You indicated to my message service that you had an urgent matter to talk to me about, so either it is not urgent anymore or whatever it was is already handled?"

Another one of those silences Rainey was use to getting when she had to deal with the bullies she occasionally had to work with in her consulting work. She just waited DC out.

"You're right. I need to get to the reason for my calling you. Do you recall last year when you were monitoring those Internet groups who make heroes out of the butchers and psychos doing multiple killings?"

"Yes."

"After you left the Bureau, I assigned one of our technicians to monitor the sites and report anything that seemed unusual or out of the ordinary. With SK having gone underground, I thought it possible she might surface in one of these groups again. Bingo. Agent Bradley brought me a short message left on a message board in one of these Internet sites. Got a pencil handy or I can email the text to you."

"Go ahead and read it and then email the text. I am traveling and can't stop to write. And don't bother to ask where I am traveling to as it is none of your business. If I think where I am is your business you will be the first to know."

DC did not argue but read,

"Thursday at 7 AM West Coast time the message said "Si! Si! Leguea Carne. Es Que."

At noon same day West Coast time the reply was, "Es Que! Donde? Si! Si!"

At 2 PM same day West Coast time the reply was, "Si! Si! Japanese Tea Garden. Saturday at 4. Es Que."

Rainey thought she had had one shock already today but this one was huge.

"Did you get that? Understand what it says?" DC asked.

"Translated, if credible, it is SK asking the Copy Cat killer to meet her and the Copy Cat killer asking where and when with SK naming the Japanese Tea Gardens. That would be tomorrow for the meeting, right?"

"You don't think it is credible?" DC asked.

"I am more interested in why you think it is. You wouldn't have raised so much hell about tracking me down if you didn't think there was at least the possibility that SK initiated a contact with the Copy Cat killer."

"True. That asshole captain called me about the Black Talon ammo surfacing in a killing in San Diego, coupled with the Copy Cat serial killer operating in LA, and now this third element; it is just too coincidental. I don't think the Copy Cat killer is SK. What bothers me is the amateurish coding of the contact message I am assuming was initiated by SK. She's just too smart to do something like that unless she has some motive we don't know about, and that wouldn't surprise me one bit either. Maybe SK is trying to say she is not the Copy Cat killer?"

"That's a possibility," Rainey said. "Did you contact the LAPD task force with this information?"

"I talked to a Captain Jenkins and he said it was a long stretch. My gut feeling is he isn't going to do anything."

"You don't think he'll set up surveillance at the meet location?" Rainey asked.

"I think the LAPD task force commander is only interested in the Copy Cat killer investigation and he doesn't give a message on a quack message board any credibility," DC replied.

"DC I gotta put you on hold a sec. Some people are waiting on me and I need to tell them I'll be a few minutes more." Rainey didn't wait for DC to reply.

Rainey walked out of the restroom and restaurant door and approached the driver's door where Ibrahim was sitting. "I am so sorry to keep you waiting. I'll finish this phone call and then be ready to leave."

"Take your time. We are not in a big hurry."

"Thanks." Rainey said, as she pushed the hold button on the phone and walked a short distance from the car.

"Still there, DC?"

"Of course I am."

"Thinking about SK's motive. Maybe she doesn't like the fact this Copy Cat is operating in LA because it's making stalking victims difficult? Maybe she doesn't like sharing media attention?" Rainey paused to hear DC's reaction.

"It's hard to know without more information. I thought it a bit strange she didn't just contact the LAPD task force. She didn't hesitate in making herself known to the task force in Arizona. Then again, it could be a couple of juveniles just messing around trying to impress each other."

Do I tell him about SK trying to contact me through my message service? Rainey hesitated. I don't want him sending the FBI to Brantlie—not yet anyways. The moment she could have said something to DC slipped away.

"Have you traced the ISPs and name-address of Si! Si! and Es Que?"

"That's in the works. You know how some of the ISPs drag their feet and we have to threaten them with Homeland Security to get information. Agent Bradley is working on that. What we do know is that the ISPs are those free services and if it is SK and the Copy Cat killer then the name and addresses are going to come back phony."

"If the addresses come back phony then I'd recontact the LAPD task force. I think you'd have enough to let them know that it's your opinion there are two known serial killers operating in their jurisdiction. Urge them to send some undercover officers to the meet site between this Es Que and Si Si."

"I am going to agree with you on this one, Rainey. I think you need to watch your back as long as you remain in the States. The sooner you wrap up your consult and join the expedition the safer you will be. SK is just too unpredictable."

"I've got to run, DC. You can reach me through my message service. I'll be checking in twice daily, and if it's an emergency, tell the service person to call me direct. Best I can do for now."

Rainey closed the phone cover and dropped the phone into her purse as she headed for the car. What had begun as a fairly simple assignment...*make myself a target and wait and see if SK goes for the bait is turning into...what?* Rainey shook her head. The days ahead stretched before Rainey and with so many uncertainties, she felt the loss of Sara deeply. She had no one to confide in as she had with Sara. Rainey got into the back seat of the car and again thanked Ibrahim and Jamilah for their patience. Rainey soon became lost in her thoughts about Arizona and what danger could be waiting for her in California.

SK

Saturday

SK woke at six AM and followed her usual routine. She made the bed, bouncing a quarter off it to be sure she wasn't getting sloppy. She dressed in her gym clothes and grabbed a bottle of water from the refrigerator. She had time for a workout at LA Fitness before coming back to the apartment, showering, and then dressing as a Muslim heathen. Today she would stop by the masjid in El Central. The once-weekly Muslim newspapers were usually distributed before the noon prayer time. SK laughed to herself. The weekly newspapers brought her more information than she could get in Arizona sitting in those boring women's groups listening to those heathens talk about their brats, recipes, and whether Abdul would get an A or B on his weekly school math test.

Running two miles to the gym each morning was something SK enjoyed. Running was about the only thing she enjoyed these days. All her careful planning. Waiting months for the surgery to heal and establishing herself in several Muslim communities had not been easy. Then that Copy Cat had to wreck everything. But she'd take care of him just like she took care of anyone keeping her from completing the mission.

You know he's making a fool out of you. "Just shut up," SK muttered to the voice. *He's taking all the credit and his kills are sloppy.*

He's making you look like a third rate chump. SK ran faster to speed up her heart rate and drown out the voice. She tossed the empty water bottle in a trash receptacle and kept running. Arriving at the fitness center, SK grabbed the door and barreled inside. She headed straight for the weight room. She dropped her apartment keys on the floor beside the leg press and began her repetitions.

Where's your old friend, Rainey? She's still walking around living her life as if nothing happened in Arizona. The voice was persistent and now the white noise began building and with it came the pain. Not even the run and working the leg press was keeping the white noise and pain at bay. It was the voice stirring things up. "I have a plan and I don't need you to rush me. If I had waited back in Arizona I would have nailed Six-of-Ten and would not be here in California having to deal with that idiot Copy Cat killer before I can take care of my own business."

"Are you talking to me?"

SK realized she had been muttering out loud and one of the fitness trainers had walked by and thought she had said something to him.

SK mustered up a rueful smile and told the man, "I'm sorry I was just thinking out loud about the tone I lost. I had to go out of town to Podunk USA and missed a couple of workouts."

"Don't ya just hate it when that happens? It always takes me a day to get back to where I was before I missed a training session. Don't be so hard on yourself. We all have to work to eat. Shit happens, if ya know what I mean."

SK nodded and pretended to be finishing up on the leg press. *It's your fault, not his. Talking out loud like that is what drew his attention to you*, the voice ridiculed her.

"Leave me alone," SK muttered softly under her breath.

I'll leave you alone when you do your duty and stop using the Copy Cat as your excuse. You still haven't found Rainey or a way to get her from the East Coast here to California.

SK could not ignore the voice. It would just increase the white noise and pain. Without finishing her workout, SK grabbed her keys from the floor and hurried out the door to the outside. She needed to run and clear her head.

SK ran the two miles back to her apartment then decided to run two extra miles before turning around and double-timing it back to the apartment. When she unlocked the front door, the voice was quiet, white noise gone, and the pain had receded. Heading for the shower, she spoke out loud, "I'll find a Six-of-Ten heathen and I'll put an end to Rainey Walker, but first things first. There's a little matter of teaching Copy Cat a lesson first."

SK dressed in a long skirt and long sleeved shirt. She put on the dark blue *abeya* and matching head scarf, but left the veil on the bedspread. "I wonder what Copy Cat has been up to. I'll visit his apartment while he's at the Japanese Tea Gardens waiting to meet me. Ha! I can't believe that idiot would fall for the same ploy twice."

SK checked her wrist watch. She had time to get the newspapers, come back and change, and do some more research before she had to be outside Jimmy-boy's penthouse apartment. She wanted to follow him to make sure he was not headed for the Tea Garden or find out if he was going to Copy Cat's apartment. *What if he did go to the apartment? Maybe both the Copy Cat and Jimmy-boy were going to the Tea Garden, with one of them the look-out? Maybe to track me once the meeting ended? Whatever. Whoever stays behind will die today. If they left Copy Cat's apartment together, then she could stay under the radar longer.* SK's only regret was that she would not be at the Tea Garden to observe Copy Cat's mounting frustration when he realized he was being stood up again.

When she went to Jimmy-boy's penthouse apartment and searched it she had realized there was something wrong with the place. It was too sterile. SK had planted the micro cameras and searched the apartment carefully, but did not find anything he would use as a weapon. No knives, guns, or ammo, and most glaringly absent were any trophies. She learned why the next day, when she followed him to another apartment complex. SK followed him to the tenth floor in a second elevator, and a Ben Franklin to the janitor led her to the information she'd been looking for.

The next morning, she called the apartment complex manager and arranged to lease an apartment on the eighth floor. Over the past weeks she passed Copy Cat several times in the building lobby, but he was always leaving the apartment, never arriving. She had followed Jimmy-boy several times to the apartment, but never saw him leaving it. She had yet to see the two men together. The Copy Cat's apartment had to be where the trophies and weapons were.

SK smiled as she looked into the mirror and adjusted the face veil. "I won't be following you tonight. I have other things I need to do. Tonight I'll visit the apartment on the tenth floor and confirm what I think about you and Jimmy-boy. Then I'm going to my storage shed." SK smiled and picked up a pair of thin, camel-hair gloves from the table and put them on.

Her good humor vanished when the gravelly voice taunted her, *What have you done to deserve a visit to the storage shed? Nothing! Six-of-Ten is still walking around somewhere, and you don't have a single target. You are fixated on the Copy Cat and his buddy, Jimmy-boy. All the while, the mission remains in limbo. You are a frickin' failure.*

"Stop it!" SK screamed at the covered face in the mirror. "The Copy Cat is going to bring Rainey Walker to California. I don't tell you everything. Now leave me alone. I have work to do."

SK picked up her purse, opened the door to her base apartment, and checked the hallway. It was empty. She closed and locked the door and walked the short distance to the Exit door that led to the stairwell, which led to the basement garage. The parking garage had an exit door to an alleyway behind the apartment building. Perfect for SK to come and go in whatever disguise she needed to wear. The new apartment she recently leased in Copy Cat's building wasn't nearly as easy to come and go from and required more planning.

Complications
Saturday - Brantlie

Rainey woke up and stretched. She opened her eyes and looked around the room. For a second she felt disoriented before recalling where she was. The small bachelor bungalow Ibrahim had told Rainey would be her home away from home while staying in Brantlie was cozy. Yes, *cozy* was the best way to describe it. The fabric of the drapes, couch, easy chair, carpeting, and bedding were in shades of brown, orange, and with accents of yellow and gold. The small kitchenette was stocked with colorful dinnerware, and the fridge had an assortment of fresh fruits, cheeses, soft drinks, fruit juices, milk, and bottled water. One of the cupboards held several boxes of whole grain cereals and crackers. Rainey was grateful for the thoughtfulness of her host family.

The keys to a two-year-old silver Kia were on the counter between the kitchenette and the rest of the living space, where Rainey's notebook and phone spent the night charging their batteries.

Rainey tossed the covers aside and headed for the bathroom. Fifteen minutes later, she was dressed and ready for a bowl of cereal and glass of fresh juice. She'd stop for coffee on her way to LA and her meeting with the Echo Team and Lieutenant Jerald.

Rainey was putting her cereal bowl away when her cell phone rang.

"Good morning, Rainey. Get a good night's sleep?'

"Hello, Jonah. The meeting still a go?"

"Does it always have to be just business, Rainey?" Jonah said softly.

Rainey's response was sharp and to the point. "Yes it does. Did you read my briefing report?" She waited while Jonah absorbed her rebuke.

"We did. We agree with your and DC's assessment of the intelligence. We should discuss this with Bob Jerald when we meet today."

"So you told him what I will be doing here in Brantlie?"

"No, not yet. He hasn't been told about your plan. Do you think he needs to know now or later?"

"If we tell him now, he's sure to take the information back to Phoenix and it will make its way back to the Bureau. And within the hour, the local Brantlie Police Department will know, and our operation will be blown before we get it off the ground. I'd rather give our plan a few days and see if I spot SK first. After what happened in Arizona, I am not going to get twisted by politics and watch the brass try to run the show according to their own agendas."

"Then we tell him what DC Britt already knows and nothing more. We let him think that we're snooping around in San Diego trying to get a line on SK. Right?"

"Pretty much. But there are a couple things I didn't tell you, or DC Britt for that matter. I intended to tell him, but the moment to do so came and went, so I just kept it to myself."

Rainey looked out the window and watched the daylight steadily chase the night shadows from the skyline.

"What's bothering you, Rainey?"

"Back in Arizona. The night you got shot and Sara and I were in the waiting room with all the other cops waiting for you to come out of surgery, Sara told me something that has been like a small splinter under the skin and only troublesome if you bump it or rub against it…know what I mean?"

"I think I do. It's there, but you don't think about it until you have reason to?"

"Something like that." Rainey answered and Jonah heard the steel creeping into her voice.

"I think you need to just say what you need to say, Rainey. I'm not made of sugar; I won't melt. If you think what you need to say is going to rain on my parade or on this operation we have undertaken, better to just say it now."

"Sara told me that when she, Lieutenant Jerald, and you got to that last intended victim's place you told the lieutenant you wanted to try to take SK alive. She said the lieutenant told you that if SK gave him the slightest reason he would blow her away. Sara wondered if you hesitated in that back yard, and that's why SK got the opportunity to put two bullets in you. The only reason you aren't dead is that she figured you were dead when she went over that back wall. I don't know, Jonah. Maybe you don't know. But I'm telling you this now. If I get the opportunity to take SK down, I am going to do it. I'm going to do whatever it takes to make sure she doesn't escape again and go underground."

Rainey listened to the labored breathing coming from Jonah through the phone receiver. She knew she had struck a chord that went deep into his psyche.

"You don't need to answer, Jonah. Like I said, I have something else I need to tell you. I know for certain the message the FBI agent found on that Internet message board was between the two serial killers. SK found my message service and left the same simple message for me three times. She spelled it out in letters, E-S space Q-U-E. SK wanted me to know that she can find me anytime and that she is coming for me wherever I am." Rainey waited as the silence seemed to stretch an unbearably long time.

"Thanks for telling me, Rainey. I know it's hard for you to trust me. I'm asking you to give me a chance. I promise that SK will not escape again if I can help it. I promise that Echo will do whatever it takes to make sure she's stopped, and if it means me taking her down, then that is what will happen."

A long silence was finally broken when Jonah asked, "Do we keep this with Echo or do we share it now with DC Britt, Lieutenant Jerald, and the LAPD Task Force?"

"If we keep it to ourselves for a while, there's a possibility that we could be charged with obstruction when it comes out, especially if something worse happens and say our holding the information created problems just like it did back in Arizona. If we clue everyone in, then our operation here in Brantlie is blown before we even have a chance to put it in motion. There's too big a chance of a leak. If SK has any idea we're setting her up in Brantlie, she could go back underground, and she could turn up anywhere in the world."

"I don't know, Rainey. Before you told me about SK calling your service, we were still speculating about that message board exchange. Now we know SK and the Copy Cat are definitely linked. For all we know, they could be helping each other, stalking victims, and hunting together."

"You, Drew, Rand and I are civilians. We are acting outside the color of the law. We don't have any protection if things go bad, and with SK, things can go really bad fast. I have a consulting contract with the Muslim communities in Arizona and California but I don't think it will hold up if the consulting work is shown to actually be an investigation and trap for SK."

"We can give them the information about SK tracking you to your message service and still keep a lid on our operation, at least for a few days, to see if that article draws SK out. While you are driving to LA I'll talk with Drew and Rand. When you get here we can decide what to do." Jonah waited for Rainey to mull over his suggestion.

"I agree. I'd like to hear what Rand and Drew think. We may have to decide on informing DC Britt, or Lieutenant Jerald or the

LAPD Task force. Whatever we decide, Rand and Drew need to know what we know and decide what they are willing to risk."

"Drive carefully. Give me a call when you get close, and I'll give you directions to our command center. We decided it was the best location for the meeting and you need to become familiar with the tools we have available."

"I can just imagine. What are you going to tell Lieutenant Jerald? He's supposed to meet with us before his plane leaves for Phoenix this afternoon."

"By the time you get here, Drew, Rand and I will have pretty much decided what we think we need to do. We'll tell you, and then all of us will decide. We can get this done before either I pick up the lieutenant for a meeting or I call him and beg off until another time."

"That sounds reasonable. I'll call you when I get to the outskirts of LA."

Rainey closed her cell phone and rested her head between her hands. She needed to see Jamilah and thank her before she left for LA. Jamilah and her children were leaving on an extended vacation today. She was the last Muslim woman in the community, or any Muslim community in California who fit SK's victim profile. She had finally given in an agreed to leave after meeting Rainey and recognizing that Rainey's alter ego Amira in their community provided an open invitation for SK to hunt. If all went as planned, Ibrahim and another Muslim man would be taking Rainey to the store tomorrow to meet her new employer if the plan didn't fall apart between now and then.

Command Center

Saturday afternoon

Rand and Drew sat on a bench attached to the side wall of the Command Center vehicle. Jonah sat on another bench on the other side of the RV. A collapsible table was setup between them. Rand was busy typing on a notebook, capturing the gist of what Jonah was telling them. Drew sat with his elbows on the table, fingers tented in front of him as he listened to Jonah.

The Command Center looked like any other RV from the outside, but the inside had been gutted to fit all the electronic equipment, computers, weapons, and sophisticated hardware Echo might need. Some of the military equipment Jonah had procured through the black market and only the military had a legal right to have access to it. The legalities did not concern Jonah or Drew and Rand. They knew what they might need for different operations and as far as Echo was concerned, the ends justified the means. Jonah made sure Echo had the means.

"Whether we continue this operation or turn it over to one of the law enforcement agencies, Jonah, I don't think it is wise to have invited this Lieutenant Jerald to meet with us here in the Command Center," Drew tossed the statement out when Jonah paused in his narrative.

Rand felt Jonah focus his attention on him, and he looked up from the computer. "I'm with Drew. From what you've told us about him he's a straight arrow. A good cop. Sharp and knows his tactical, but seems like he doesn't have many grey areas, and the Command Center could hardly be called a grey area. Cops will see it as something they'd want to inventory and impound, and lock us up to boot!"

Jonah gave a deep laugh and even Drew grinned. Rand wasn't too far off the mark.

"Jonah, it doesn't matter if we stick with this operation or not. There will be other operations and we need to keep a lid on this command center. No matter what gets decided, any meeting you have with the lieutenant needs to be anywhere else but here."

"I agree with Drew. I don't think anybody other than Rainey needs to know about Echo and I am not up for meeting any cops, even if they are the good guys."

Jonah looked at his partners and slowly nodded his head in agreement. "Then that's settled. If Rainey wants to turn over the information she gets from the Muslim communities and the information about SK contacting her and the bulletin board, verifying the connection between her and the Copy Cat killer, we ask her to leave Echo out of it. Agreed?"

Rand and Drew nodded agreement.

"What about the Brantlie operation?" Drew asked.

"It was Rainey's idea and she set things up with the Muslim communities. If she wants to blow the whistle on it then it's her call. If she wants to leave it out of any information sharing with the cops then I vote we stick with her and push forward with the operation," Rand replied.

"What about you, Drew? Do you go along with Rand or have something else to say on this?"

"We planned to go after SK with or without Rainey. I was against involving her at first, but she's turned out to be a real asset. She's a smart ex-cop, got good instincts, and I trust her. That said, Echo is going after SK with or without her. If she blows the whistle, we just fade to the background and move our operation forward without her."

"I agree with Drew. When she gets here, you do the talking, Jonah. Once we know what she has decided, and she will have decided before she gets here, we can take our cue from that point. You can then call Lieutenant Jerald and meet with him or cancel your meeting, if that's the way the wind is going to blow."

"Ya know what I have been thinking partners?" Jonah looked from Rand to Drew. "I think Echo should try to take out two serial killers in this operation before we pack it in and leave for the East Coast."

Rand and Drew nodded at Jonah. The three men got up from the benches and headed for the front door of the command center. Now that their staff meeting was over they had nothing to do for a change but sit outdoors in the canvas chairs, relax, and wait for Rainey to arrive.

Rainey looked at the rows of RVs and trailers as she turned into the Shady Rest Travel Park. The park seemed to be divided into two sections. On the right of the main 'street' the smaller RVs and trailers were parked in neat rows and to her left the larger motor homes and trailers were parked. Up ahead she saw a pink trailer with a large sign hanging from a window with the word 'Office' lit up in bright red neon lights.

Rainey turned left at the second lane and at the end she saw three men sitting in canvas lawn chairs outside a large, white RV. The men were drinking something in tall glasses that dripped with condensation from the ice and heat outside the glasses. Rainey's parched throat salivated as she pulled into a parking slot next to the RV.

The three men stood as Rainey got out of her car and approached. Three men couldn't have looked more different than the Echo team standing and greeting her with warm smiles.

Rainey turned her attention to Rand first. She held out her hand. "Hello Rand. Nice to meet you."

Rand extend his right arm and shook hands with Rainey. "It's nice to meet you, too, Rainey."

"Drew. Jonah. Thanks for the great directions. I didn't get lost more than a couple of times and I'm only five minutes late," Rainey grinned at the three men and the atmosphere seemed to melt and relax.

"How about a glass of fresh brewed iced tea?" Jonah offered, and Rainey smiled her acceptance and sat down in his chair. Jonah raised an eyebrow, but didn't say anything as he went inside the RV to get Rainey's iced tea. Jonah's chair was *his* chair as Drew and Rand both knew. They both smirked at Jonah as he had walked by them.

Jonah returned carrying the tea in one hand and a metal folding chair. He handed the tea to Rainey and then unfolded the chair and sat down next to Rand. "Aren't we missing someone?" Rainey asked after taking a large gulp of the tea.

"Maybe and maybe not," Jonah replied. "Let's take a few minutes to enjoy the tea and let you unwind from your drive. Then we can adjourn to the command center and talk." Rainey nodded and allowed her muscles to relax and savor her tea.

Rainey drained the last of her tea when her cell phone rang. "Excuse me while I answer this."

"Go ahead and stay put. We're going inside. When you finish your call, come and join us," Jonah said as the three men stood up and began walking the short distance to the command center door.

"Salaams Zarinah. Yes, I got here okay and I'm meeting with Jonah and his team right now."

"Salim called and told me they published an announcement about you, or should I say Amira, visiting in Brantlie for the summer. That kind of bait is pretty obvious don't you think?"

"If SK has been busy trying to track down a potential victim, she will latch onto that article. We don't know if she is hunting in California for sure, Zarinah. Remember we are just hoping to smoke her out of hiding and make it irresistible for her to ignore the opportunity to stalk the prime and only victim available."

"I know what you say is the way it's gotta be done, I just wanted to hear your voice and let you know that everyone in the community is praying for your safety. Just keep in touch with me, please. Your grandmother would never forgive me if some harm comes to you."

"I promised to call regularly and I will. Now stop worrying so much. I gotta get back to the meeting. Salaams and love ya."

"As salaam'alaykum Rainey and we love you, too."

Rainey opened the door to the command center and saw a typical captain's seat on the driver's side. Her jaw dropped in amazement, though, when she opened the partition to the back. Rainey stood in the doorway and tried hard to keep her amazement in check.

"Come on in and join us Rainey." Jonah motioned to the padded bench he was sitting on across from Rand and Drew. Above the benches on either side of the RV were computer and television screens. Rainey saw three notebooks hooked into electrical outlets on the table. Beyond the table and benches were what looked to be large drawers built into the walls of the next section of the RV. She could see what looked like four doors to rooms beyond that area towards the back of the RV.

"The first door on the right is the all important bathroom that has a small but serviceable shower. The first door on the left is the weapons room. The very last door on the left is where we have two motorcycles stored with helmets and gear packed in the saddlebags on each. The last room on the right is what Rand calls his lab. He can do some very basic forensic analysis if we need it done and it can't wait."

Rainey just nodded her head trying to take it all in. She looked at an unfamiliar piece of equipment on the bench next to Drew. "What's that?" Rainey asked pointing at the equipment.

Jonah's eyes followed the direction to where Rainey had pointed. "You don't need to know the name, Rainey. It's used as a listening device. As long as there's a window and a warm body inside that little honey will pick up anything said in a room and record the conversation. You can be a mile away and use that device and still pick up the sound of a rat crossing a floor."

Rainey raised her eyebrows. "I've never seen a device like that and the FBI has some pretty sophisticated equipment used for a similar purpose, but without that kind of range. Of course a listening device is used only with a legally executed warrant."

"Of course," Jonah said, and did his best to smother his grin.

Rainey sat down next to Jonah. Drew slid an open notebook across the table to her. "Rand has summarized the situation and possible alternatives. Please read what he has typed on the screen and tell us what you think for each bullet point."

These guys look so loose and relaxed but are they ever efficient! Rainey thought as she looked down at the screen now in front of her.

Point 1 – If we choose to notify any law enforcement agency it should be Rainey doing the notification and the most logical choice is DC Britt.

Point 2 – Rainey tells DC Britt about SK's messages left with her message service. It's then his call to notify the LAPD Task Force.

Point 3 – Echo thinks Lieutenant Jerald should be notified by Jonah at a separate meeting, not at the Command Center. If we don't tell him, we run the risk of alienating him but it can't be helped.

Point 4 – Echo thinks Rainey should tell DC Britt about the Muslims moving all the SK target profile Muslim women and their families out of California and about the community ban on anyone mentioning their absence or discussing Iraq even among them.

Point 5 – Echo will accept any decision Rainey makes reference notifying law enforcement about the Brantlie operation or not notifying them.

"I agree with Echo on Points 1 through 4, but on Point 5, let's hold off letting law enforcement know about our operation at least for a few days so we can see if SK takes the bait. Zarinah told me the Amira story has published in the *Brantlie Muslim Voice* today and it's likely if SK reads the story she'll be headed to Brantlie to begin stalking Amira."

"Then you want to go ahead with the operation without bringing any of the law enforcement agencies into it?" Rand asked. He was surprised that Rainey would choose this option.

Drew wasn't surprised. He'd spent enough time with Rainey to know she'd want to stick to her plan. She wanted to find SK worse than Jonah did.

"Eventually they are going to be in the thick of this, but I want to have at least a chance at identifying her before we call in reinforcements." Rainey replied.

"Don't forget that we don't know how SK's relationship with the Copy Cat will figure into our operation. He might go to Brantlie and work with SK," Drew said.

"It's just so out of character for SK to become buddy-buddy with someone with the Copy Cat's profile." Jonah stated what Rainey was thinking.

"There's something happening that we just don't know about. The real unknown in this situation. We know SK wants to take out Rainey and kill number six-of-ten. So why is she messing around with this other serial killer?" Rand tossed out to the others.

"One of us is going to have to stay in LA and sniff around for intelligence. Maybe if we get a line on the Copy Cat it would help us track SK," Drew said.

"That's a big maybe." Jonah said. "But I agree that two of us need to stay in Brantlie and keep track of Rainey while one of us needs to stay in LA."

"I think it's a mistake to blow off Lieutenant Jerald. He's been our inside man with the Copy Cat task force. He doesn't want to go back to Phoenix. He also thinks SK is here in LA," Rand said.

"True enough. He is hoping his meeting with me today will give him something to convince his supervisors he should stay in LA, and he needs something to convince the task force that he's needed as a member," Jonah replied.

"If Jonah gives the same info to Lieutenant Jerald that I give to DC Britt and both of them contact the LAPD, then their information would have double credibility with the task force," Rainey suggested.

Jonah looked at the team sitting with him at the table. The other three members nodded their heads in agreement with him. "Then it's decided. Rainey calls DC Britt and I call Jerald and get him to delay or cancel his flight and I meet with him. So I guess Drew gets to stay in LA and I go to Brantlie after I meet with Bob Jerald. Rand and Rainey return to Brantlie together."

Rainey's cell phone rang. "Excuse me while I take this call." Rainey turned her back toward the three men.

Jonah nodded, did the same thing, and flipped the cover of his cell phone and speed dialed Lieutenant Jerald. "Hello Bob. Sorry for the delay. Yes, I know your flight leaves in thirty minutes, but I have some information that I think credible enough to get you a ticket back into the Copy Cat task force."

A slow smile spread across Jonah's face as he listened to the lieutenant talking. "Okay. I can be at the airport in twenty minutes, but I can't get through all the gate keepers in time. Remember I'm not carrying a badge anymore. Yes what I have to tell you is good enough to justify cancelling your flight. I'll meet you in the airport lounge on the second level. Okay. I'll see you shortly."

Jonah had turned his back to the group at the table so Rainey would be less disturbed when answering her phone call. When he turned back to the group he noticed Drew and Rand had a keyed-up look. Their adrenalin was pumping. Rainey looked like she had been kicked in the gut. She was pale and her fingers were balled into tight fists.

"What's happened, Rainey? Who called you?" Jonah asked with a hard edge to his voice.

Rand turned his notebook toward Jonah. "Rainey's answering service called her and Rainey had the service send the urgent message to her at my email address."

"Go ahead and read it, Jonah." Rainey said.

Jonah started: "Today's date EDT 7:30 PM. The caller identified herself as Es Que. She spelled out the name as follows: E-S space Q-U-E. She then said, quote: 'This is an urgent call for Rainey Walker. Visited Si Si's apartment. He has terrible taste in decorations. I'd like to show it to you. ES QUE.' Rainey, she didn't give me time to answer. She hung up immediately after she said the word 'you.' I wasn't able to ask her for a phone number per your instructions. Sorry. Janice at 24/7."

"Hmm...7:30 PM eastern daylight time means SK called at about 4:30 PM here in California or ten minutes ago," Rainey said.

"She wants to show you the Copy Cat's apartment?" Jonah asked with raised eyebrows.

"I feel sort of sick, but I think she has to be referring to Copy Cat's trophies. There's been nothing in the media so LAPD is probably holding back this information." Rainey's taut face matched the sound of her voice.

Rand nodded agreement and asked Rainey, "Do you think she's threatening you?"

Before Rainey could answer Drew spoke up, "Naw, that psycho wants to lure Rainey out to LA. Right now she doesn't know where Rainey is, so she's giving her just enough information to motivate Rainey to come to SK's hunting grounds. She wants to stalk Rainey, but on her terms, with all the advantages."

"I agree with that assessment, Drew. I also think SK plans to cut and run and go underground as soon as she can make a Six-of-Ten kill and destroy Rainey." Jonah again got nodding agreement from the Echo team.

Rainey squared her shoulders and looked at the men. "I think it's time for me to call DC Britt and it's time for Jonah to get moving towards the airport. I brought some city maps, courtesy of the Muslim imams and a floor plan of the store I'll be working in as Amira. My temporary uncle drew up a plan of his home and the bungalows. There is a phone number for a rental car dealership. Just say Rainey Walker and you can get a vehicle anytime to use. We'll leave a copy with you, Drew. The command center stays here or goes to Brantlie?"

"It goes to Brantlie with Rand. He'll let you know its location when he gets there," Jonah said.

"Give me an hour before calling DC. That way he gets the information about the same time as I'm giving it to Bob Jerald. You might suggest that DC put a tap on your messenger service, but I doubt if anything would come of that. SK is using either throwaways or public phones. She doesn't stay on the line long enough for a regular trace, but with some of the new military hardware maybe..." Jonah's voice trailed off.

Rainey, Rand, and Drew grinned at Jonah. The tension dissipated as the Echo team began preparations to get on the road.

"Let's all keep in touch," were Jonah's parting words as he drove away from the command center and headed for LAX.

James E. Thornton III

After the first no-show meeting between the Copy Cat and SK, she followed Thornton to his penthouse apartment in Thornton Towers. *Why did the Copy Cat send Thornton in his place? Who is Thornton, and who is Christopher Carrington, and how are they connected?* SK had made it her business to learn everything she could about James E. Thornton. Christopher Carrington was more elusive and more difficult to peg.

SK tracked down Thornton's elderly housekeeper in a retirement home. The old woman had worked for the Thorntons and had been pensioned off recently after the death of Jimmy-boy's mother. SK learned what she needed to know about Jimmy-boy after spending several days becoming the old woman's new best friend by volunteering at the retirement home twice a week. While SK brushed the old woman's thinning hair, the old woman talked non-stop about her years in the service of the high and mighty Thorntons. SK let her run on and on. The old woman spoke with such venom about the grandson Jimmy-boy, whom she hated with a passion. SK had no doubt that after working for the family for forty years, the old woman knew all the family secrets and skeletons in the closet. SK didn't doubt for a minute that the old woman had spied on the family and became the confidant of Jimmy-boy's mother on many occasions.

At age twenty-two, James E.Thornton III, grandson of a Wall Street financier and son of Thornton Allied Industries CEO, graduated from Harvard. His family had big plans for James, and James had big plans for James that did not include his family. After spending a decade of jaunting from country to country and spending money as fast as he drank premium wines and liquors, James had returned six months ago from Europe to Los Angeles.

The old woman told SK that Jimmy-boy's mother had said, "Every young man needs to travel and gain a worldview and understanding." The mother made this excuse for him to her friends while waiting and hoping for his return. But time ran out for Vivian Thornton, as she died of cervical cancer waiting for her son to come home. James had not returned to the States for his mother's funeral. His mother had left him a sizeable inheritance regardless of his deserting her. The old woman said that after Vivian died, his father had made it clear to James through the family attorney that James was disinherited for the pain and suffering he had caused his mother.

"Why did you dislike James so much when he was growing up? I don't understand that. I understand about disliking him for not coming back to see his mother when she was so ill." SK had asked innocently enough although the point was to bait the woman to tell all.

The old woman said that James had not bothered to respond to his father's anger when he was a teenager, nor did he as an adult. He showed up at the family mansion ten years to the day after stealing money and his mother's jewelry from his father's safe and leaving for Europe. Upon his return, his grandfather received him with open arms as the prodigal son. His father, without saying a word, left the room and the house. James did not care that his father had ignored him; that was nothing new for James.

SK held on to her patience as she prodded the old woman some more. "You said his father is still angry with him. That doesn't explain your dislike of the young Jimmy?"

The old woman needed no urging to let go of the Thornton family secret, and a good one it was. It seems that James began killing when he was ten years old. His first victim was his mother's favorite cat. Soon after, one by one, the rest of her cats disappeared. Next the parakeets with broken necks were found in their cages, and the twenty-gallon aquarium was drained and the fish left to die in the waterless tank. When James was thirteen he was vacationing with his mother at their summer home and one evening he decided to take the family dog for a walk. James had just slit the collie's throat and had the knife poised to gut the dog when his father's thunderous voice yelled his name. James dropped the knife and took off. After spending the night hiding in the boat house, at dawn he went back to the house and crept through the kitchen, hoping he could get to his mother before his father found him. "I heard them, the Mister and Missus arguing something terrible about the killing of them animals, and then that same day he came home the Mister stormed out of the house."

"Then what happened?" SK prompted.

"The Missus walked out of the library and saw James climbing the staircase and called out to him. Before he could tell another one of his big lies, the Missus with her usual whine, told him that he had missed seeing his father, who had to leave immediately because of an urgent business matter. The Missus didn't mind telling her own lies and didn't seem to have noticed James had been out all night, or maybe she just pretended not to notice? James and his father only agreed on one thing: that she was a weak-minded narcissist who clung to James like an oily vine."

"My, that is really awful!" SK pretended to be shocked. "Didn't his father or grandfather ever talk to James about killing the family pets? Did they get him counseling?" SK had asked.

The old hag just shook her head and said, "No one but James and his father seemed to notice, or if they did, they never said anything about the dead animals or how they avoided each other. The fact that there weren't more family pets after the collie disappeared seems to have fanned the flames of James' hatred for his father."

On another visit, the old woman told SK that the butler at the grandfather's home kept in touch with her and he had come to visit her after James came home from Europe. The butler told her that within two weeks of his homecoming, James made it clear to his grandfather that he would never work for or with his father in Thornton–Allied Industries. His grandfather, however, retained a controlling interest in Thorndyne Pharmaceutical also headquartered in Los Angeles. James was made a Senior VP, providing him a penthouse apartment and a senior executive corporate office. What he was supposed to do at his new and first place of employment wasn't spelled out. James did not care enough to ask.

After listening to the old woman SK knew, or thought she knew, what Jimmy-boy and the Copy Cat had in common.

SK's investigation of James E. Thornton III led her to Thorndyne Pharmaceutical where she made friends with Jimmy-boy's executive secretary. SK met the secretary in the employee cafeteria by striking up a casual conversation that led to inviting the secretary to a premier opening of one of the hottest movies to come out this year. SK took the secretary to one of Hollywood's swankiest dinner clubs afterwards for a bite to eat and the secretary was only too eager to talk about the boss she secretly despised as a rich good-for-nothing.

The secretary told SK that her boss gave her and everyone the creeps. Oh, he could be charming when he wanted to be, but most of the time he was just 'cold' and she thought he was plain evil. She didn't know why, but she was glad he rarely showed up at the work place.

She said he attended required executive meetings to keep his grandfather happy, and he checked in occasionally with her to sign papers, but that was the extent of any work involvement. Jimmy-boy's boss took one look at the cold emptiness he saw in

James' eyes and steered clear of him. If James wanted to show up now and then, fine. If not, that was fine, too. His boss was relieved when James made it clear he was not to be bothered.

The other VPs and department heads were surprised when James and one of the senior accountants began hanging around together. James went out of his way to be his most charming with the accountant. A month after James started working at the pharmaceutical company, the accountant emailed a resignation without any notice or explanation. James made no effort to explain the accountant's strange actions to any of the other VPs or employees and claimed he was just as surprised as everyone else by the sudden resignation of the accountant. The accountant just happened to be Christopher Carrington, who SK thought was the Copy Cat killer.

SK

Saturday afternoon

"As Salaam 'Alaykum," SK said to the man handing out copies of the weekly Muslim newspaper. *How stupid can they be? Publishing newspapers and then giving them away free. No wonder most of the Muslims were always broke. They don't have an ounce of business sense.*

SK kept her covered head and veiled face lowered as she walked slowly out of the mosque entry lobby. The Muslim women were coming out of the mosque from a side door and were congregating in the courtyard. Some were scolding young children who were playing tag. The men had all come out from prayer using the front door. SK had tried to become friendly with several of the women over the last three months, but every time she mentioned the dearly departed sisters who were so cruelly slain in Arizona last year, all she got was the women immediately beginning to recite their dua prayers.

SK didn't bother approaching any of the women today. She was on a tight schedule and wanted to get home and comb the Muslim newspapers before she went to visit Copy Cat 's apartment while he was busy across town at the Japanese Tea Gardens looking for her. If he got mad at being stood up again and left right away, she had a good hour or more to search. If he waited around or went looking for her, she'd have two hours or more, given LA traffic. If Jimmy-boy showed up at the apartment, he'd get his throat cut as a present for the Copy Cat once he returned from being stood up again by SK.

Struck out again. You think reading those papers is going to help you locate Six-of-Ten. Ha! Why are you being so picky? Any one of those heathen women would do, the voice taunted SK as she parked the SUV in her space in the underground parking lot.

"I have a mission and purpose. Fat chance you'd understand that. You're just like the Copy Cat. Ignorant. He kills because he loves to kill. He doesn't have to have a reason or purpose."

But he gets the job done. You haven't done anything to advance the mission since you took out that doctor months ago, the voice sneered.

The pain was at a low buzz and the white noise was keeping pace. "Don't get angry," SK muttered out loud.

Still going to the shed to visit your trophies? What good are they, if you have to keep them in some dark building hidden away? If you kept them here at the apartment like you did in the house in Arizona, we could enjoy them every day. You making them some kind of reward is just denying us both pleasure, the voice had turned soft and silky. SK hated the voice even more when it tried to use temptation to get its way.

"Just leave me alone. I have too much to do, and your friends only make things worse and disrupt my concentration."

Hey, they're your friends. You invite them every time you blow up about something. Don't blame me, the voice whined. SK did not bother to answer the voice.

She got out of the SUV. Carrying the stack of papers and plastic bag with the Muslim clothing, she looked around, making sure no one was around to notice her. SK opened the door to the stairwell and entered it. She climbed the stairs to the second floor landing, opened the door and entered the hallway.

Inside the apartment, she scanned the room checking to ensure that the traps she had set for unwanted visitors were all undisturbed. Breathing a sigh of relief, SK took a cold bottle of water and a piece of fruit from the fridge and made her way to her bedroom where she stretched herself across the bed and began looking carefully at the Muslim newspapers. She was searching for any names or references to Muslims from Iraq. Birth Announcements and Community Events were usually the sections with the most information.

SK finished eating the apple and drained the water bottle. It was after one o'clock. "I'll finish the papers and spend some time on the Internet. I've got plenty of time to get to Jimmy-boy's penthouse and watch him drive to the apartment complex or to the meeting..."

SK's voice trailed off as her eyes spotted the article on the third page of the *Brantlie Muslim Voice*. SK sat up and read the article intently. She read it a second time and then began to smile.

"And you said I was wasting my time reading Muslim newspapers," SK shouted out loud in her glee. The voice remained silent.

SK wanted to throw some clothes in a suitcase, grab her murder kit, and take off for Brantlie immediately, but her training and experience pushed down hard and helped her calm down.

SK looked at the face in the mirror over the dresser drawers and continued her conversation. "You've got some loose ends to tie up here in LA first, and you need to do some research about the town of Brantlie and the Muslim community there. You'll need to learn the landmarks, find the place this Amira will be staying, and create a cover story to use while stalking the heathen."

SK turned on the computer and clicked on the Internet. In the search engine she typed Brantlie California. First item up was a business directory sponsored by the Chamber of Commerce. SK clicked the link. Scanning the page her eyes stopped and she placed the cursor over the hyperlink and clicked. "My, what a nice little community," she sneered as she began reading. She picked up her cell phone and dialed the number listed.

SK waited until the woman stopped speaking. "Good afternoon. My name is Elaine Stewart and I am calling on behalf of my mother. My father passed just a year ago and the house has become too large and difficult for my mother living alone. Thank you. I appreciate your kind words. Mom is looking for a quiet community where she can still maintain her independence, but have the special services she might need. I saw the advertisement on the Internet and your community looks just like what she is looking for."

SK waited while the woman went on and on and during a pause, SK continued, "Yes, she is disabled but still drives. She has a specially outfitted van." SK waited for the woman to dribble on some more. "I see. Well, mother will feel right at home. I'll talk to her and perhaps we could stop by for a tour and look at the bungalow you have available. Yes. I'll call back as soon as I talk to mother. Why not Tuesday, at say, elevenish?" SK waited again for the blabber mouth to finish gushing. "We will see you then on Tuesday."

SK closed the cover to the cell phone and clicked off the Internet. Now her plan was beginning to have form. Her heart beat faster as a feeling of excitement enveloped her. She was on the hunt at last! She looked at herself in the mirror and spoke, "No voice? No white noise or pain? I told you I had a plan and things would come together." Silence greeted her and she turned from the mirror and opened the large handbag on the bed. Quickly she checked the contents inside, satisfied that she was ready for a fun evening doing recon at Copy Cat's apartment.

Copy Cat

Saturday morning

James slowly came to consciousness. He had made it back to his penthouse apartment at almost 4 AM after a small detour in his plans. That nosey cab driver had been the blood lust release he needed, but it had delayed him. After the kill, he went to Christopher's apartment to change before he could go back to the penthouse. Once home, he powered up the computer and Internet and checked the message board. He swallowed his disappointment when there was no new message from SK. He fell into bed as the physical exhaustion and the adrenalin burn from the kill took its toll.

James rubbed his eyes and thought about the previous evening. It wasn't as much fun as playing with Dee-Dee would have been, but the sheer audacity of the cabbie murder with all its unknowns, and the fear that had pushed him as he jogged to that bus stop had been enough to take the edge off his blood lust. James suddenly felt a surge of energy. Today he would be meeting SK. He felt sure she would not stand the Copy Cat up again. *Maybe she left the Copy Cat a message this morning?*

James got out of his king-sized bed, letting the silk sheets drop away from his naked body. He walked out to the living room and opened the notebook on the glass coffee table. A red light was blinking, letting him know he had email or voice mail waiting.

He ignored the waiting messages and powered-up the Internet, logging onto the message board. Scrolling down he looked for a message from SK.

James let out a whoop and holler. There it was. She'd left a message! "SI! SI! c-u @ 4. Es Que."

James reread the short message. His stomach growled. He was hungry now. Things were looking up. He couldn't wait to broach his idea to SK. He had thought about it on the bus ride to Christopher's, then later as he drove to the penthouse.

His palms began to sweat and he began to feel the need for sexual relief that only comes with the blood lust release. To distract himself, James hit the voice messages from the day before and listened to his secretary pass on the messages he would have heard had he been to the office in the last week.

Message 1:

"Mr. Thornton, Mr. James E.Thornton, your grandfather, has telephoned three times this past week. The last message he gave me today he said was urgent. He has arranged a family business dinner at his estate for Sunday evening at eight. He said he expects you and your father to attend as there is an urgent business matter to discuss which will impact both you and your father. Mr. Thornton said he would love for you to come early so you and he had time to relax and talk about pleasantries."

Message 2:

"A mandatory meeting for all VPs and Senior Director's with the CEO is scheduled for Monday at nine AM sharp. There will be a video-teleconference with your grandfather during the meeting. The memo said attendance is not discretionary. The memo is signed by the CEO."

Message 3:

"I took the liberty of having a signature stamp created for your name. Paperwork comes into the office and because of your extensive travel you are not always available to sign these documents. I attend all meetings as your representative and am familiar with almost all documents sent to you for signature. I hope I have not over-stepped my place in providing this assistance to you."

The last message made James smile. His secretary was sharp and had an eye for self promotion and using opportunities to her advantage. Nothing wrong with that as long as James was benefiting. *My extensive travel? Soon, but first Grandfather's family dinner.* James visualized his secretary. When he met her that first day he reported for work, he immediately thought of the pleasure he'd have watching the life die in her beautiful violet eyes. Now he was elated that his decision to keep work and play separate had paid off big time. His secretary needed a raise. A big one, to keep her loyalty a while longer. When he had full control of his inheritance he wouldn't need the job or the secretary. *Maybe then I'll have some playtime with her?*

His grandfather's family dinner would be about the mandatory company meeting on Monday. If the company was in financial trouble, James just might have to help his grandfather out of the crisis and out of this world. James could liquidate any assets and transfer the money to his Swiss account or the one he had in the Caribbean. Things might have cooled down in Europe and he could return. He really preferred the lifestyle of the Europeans, and hunting in Europe was so much more challenging, given the different languages, customs, and personas he had to create to operate successfully.

James erased the messages and deleted all emails without bothering to read them. He closed the notebook and flipped open his cell phone. "Duty calls," he chuckled as he dialed his grandfather.

James ordered a huge brunch from the onsite kitchen. His meal arrived and he ate and daydreamed about his meeting with the famous SK. He would need to leave about two-thirty in order to get ready at Christopher's place. *I think I'll drive the Bentley. Perhaps it will impress her?*

SK

Saturday late afternoon

SK parked the SUV across the street and sat watching the entrance to the parking garage of the apartment complex. She followed Jimmy-boy from the penthouse. He was driving a late-model dark blue Caddy. The lazy parking garage attendant was busy reading a *Penthouse* magazine and barely looked up as James drove through the entrance, parked the Caddy in the space next to the silver Bentley, and hurried to the service elevator.

SK waited until the elevators closed, then drove the SUV into the parking garage and parked in her own parking space. She settled back and waited. Copy Cat would be stepping out of that elevator within forty-five minutes if he was going to be on time for his meeting at the Japanese Tea Gardens. Jimmy-boy would be with Copy Cat if he had any idea what it would cost him to stay behind.

SK waited patiently, anticipating what she would find in apartment number 1041 on the tenth floor. She didn't think she would find the man whose name was on the lease for that apartment. She kept an eye on the elevator and forty minutes later she heard the chime of the elevator and the doors open. A tall, well-muscled young man in his mid-thirties, with curly dark hair just a tad long in the back stepped out of the elevator. He was dressed in a grey light-weight Armani casual suit, silver silk shirt, and dark grey tie with thin red stripes. His Gucci shoes were shined to mirror perfection. Car key in one hand, he walked toward the silver Bentley.

SK opened her large leather bag and took out a miniature camera. She wanted to get a picture of Copy Cat on his way to his meeting at the Japanese Tea Garden. She noticed the elegantly dressed man carried a small leather case that he tossed into the front passenger seat as he got into the Bentley. SK smirked, thinking about the look on his face when she was a no-show again. She'd have to wait a few minutes to see if Jimmy-boy was going to leave, or if he was another detail she would have to take care of before she did her search of the apartment. How much could she taunt Copy Cat before he turned on her and decided to try and track her down and kill her in a rage? *Try...fat chance he'd get*. Rage... yes that is what she wanted Copy Cat to feel, because rage caused mistakes and she wanted him making mistakes. She wanted to see what he would do when he found Jimmy-boy dead!

SK waited ten minutes but Jimmy-boy failed to appear in the garage. "So be it," she spoke aloud, and decided to try the phone to see if Jimmy-boy answered. She took the elevator up to the lobby. She smiled at the desk clerk and pointed at the phone. Taking the phone, she dialed Christopher's number. The phone rang ten times without a human or machine picking up.

SK took the elevator up to the eighth floor to her own apartment. She needed to think. Something was bubbling on the surface and she needed to grasp it before she moved on to Christopher's apartment. SK smiled when it came to her.

She took a large cloth shopping bag from her bedroom closet and filled it with the necessary tools she would need, then left the apartment and took the elevator to the tenth floor.

Getting inside the apartment was a piece of cake. He foolishly had not taken many precautions, thinking his hide out would never be found by the LAPD task force. The upscale apartment complex had an excellent reputation for being almost burglary free, and was sought after mostly by yuppies and mid-level business executives. The twenty story building offered a fully equipped gym, health bar, and Olympic sized pool. SK regretted her inability to spend any time in the gym.

SK pulled on her protective gloves as she walked down to room 1041 and knocked on the door and waited. She checked the door for markers that Copy Cat might have left to identify intruders in his absence. She found none. She knocked again and waited. No response, as she expected. SK reached into the large handbag and took out the stolen duplicate key card for room 1041 and inserted it. She slowly pushed the door open. All was quiet and dark in the room. The living room drapes were closed shutting out any sunlight. A musty smell permeated the air. SK felt for the light switch and found it to the right of the door.

SK felt the emptiness of the apartment. She walked through each room quickly to be sure, starting with the kitchen. The refrigerator's contents were covered with mold and stunk. She quickly closed the door. The guest bedroom, living room, and dining area were covered with a thick layer of dust. A cloud of dust erupted as she looked out a window as dozens of dust motes flew into the room. She pulled the drapes shut.

She walked back to the master bedroom door and pushed it completely open. Here the room was clean and she saw fresh linens on the bed. The dresser was dusted, too. She peered in the large bathroom and noted wet towels hanging out of a hamper, signaling that the bathroom had been used recently, and a stack of clean towels and wash cloths were on a shelf. Toiletries for a male littered the vanity.

SK walked back to the five-drawer dresser and began opening the drawers. Jackpot. One drawer was full of men's wigs, another held a professional makeup kit, and in the bottom drawer was a curious round crystal jar with a lid and a thick fluid inside... about three-fourths full. "Interesting," she thought aloud.

She closed the drawers carefully, making sure she had not disturbed any intrusion markers. There were none. Next, SK walked over to the first of the two walk-in style closets. Flipping the light switch inside, she saw the closet was full of men's shirts, shoes, pants, several business suits, a rack with several dozen different ties hanging on it, and built-ins to hold men's tee shirts, underwear, socks, and athletic clothing. She closed the door after turning off the light.

SK walked to the second walk-in closet and turned the door knob. Nothing happened. The door was locked. SK's lips curved into a sly grin. She got on her knees and examined the built in lock. She reached into her handbag and pulled out the black kit with lock-picking tools and went to work. In seconds the door was unlocked and opened. SK flipped the light switch and let out a howl of glee.

"Ah, there they are! Copy Cat's trophies!" SK was elated with her find. Along the back wall of the closet was what looked to be a cedar display case with purple velvet covering the two shelves. On the shelves were round crystal jars filled with the same kind of thick liquid she had seen in the crystal jar in the dresser drawer. The jars on the shelves were not empty. In each jar was a body part perfectly preserved. *That's what the liquid is...a preservative!* SK shuddered while being drawn towards the back of the large closet and to the crystal jars. As she approached, the display case lit up, bathing the jars in a soft light and causing the crystal to sparkle and glitter colored prisms.

A bronze plaque with an engraved date was placed in front of each crystal jar. Three were from the Copy Cat's most recent kills. He had apparently taken the pinkie finger of each of his prey, as well as other random body parts. This information had been withheld by the police and not reported in the news. SK was fascinated and repulsed at the same time. She counted the crystal jars. There were a total of fifteen. Some had ears that appeared to be pickled inside the liquid. One ear still had a gem stud in it. Others held body organs and one jar held a pair of eyes staring out from the liquid surrounding them.

SK said to herself with begrudging awe, "Damn! Copy Cat has been a busy boy. Fifteen years! He would have been just seventeen-years-old when he made his first kill. Hmm, why haven't any of these killings surfaced in the news?" Another thought struck SK. *Why had he decided to make himself a celebrity by doing poor imitation copycat killings in LA after killing twelve people totally under the radar of law enforcement?* SK turned from the display case mounted on the wall and began to survey the small room. Jimmy-boy taking on the persona of a copycat killer now puzzled her. Impersonating the man whose name was on the apartment lease was another mystery. She had considered him a poor imitation wannabe, but all this?

Copy Cat isn't the dummy you thought he was, the voice sneered.

"Shut up!"

SK couldn't resist her impulse. She took one of the crystal jars holding a pinkie finger and carefully placed it in her purse. She took out her camera and took pictures of the trophy case and other shelves in the closet, as well as a small work bench and equipment. There were cases containing various types of knives, pistols, and revolvers. One shelf was dedicated to small bottles of powders and liquids. SK took a quick look and identified several lethal poisons. She looked at three heavily stickered steamer trunks placed next to the opposite wall from the weapons. The locks were open and on lifting the lids, SK found all three empty. *No Christopher Carrington in there*, she giggled. *He was doing a fairly good job of convincing the security, janitors, management, and his lovely ladies that Christopher Carrington was alive and well. What had Jimmy-boy done with Mr. Carrington?*

SK felt a shiver of revulsion at the extent of Jimmy-boy's twist-ed lust for blood. She glanced at her wrist watch and knew she had to leave this pit of hell. *Hypocrite. Why are you pretending such distain and shock? You would think you'd never killed and destroyed a life.* The gravelly voice taunted SK. *Jimmy-boy's as smart as they come, maybe smarter than you! Even had you fooled for awhile, didn't he?* The voice continued to rant.

"I don't kill for the joy of it or blood lust. I've killed to avenge my military brothers and their families!" SK yelled at the taunting voice.

You've enjoyed every second of it, the voice continued. *The doctors who helped you. What about that cop in Phoenix? And you try to justify the killings as a necessary means to the ends. Collateral damage is what you call them,* the voice came back louder, and with it, the white noise bubbled and the pain caused her eyes to twitch. *And what about your dear friend Rainey Walker? Was that any way to treat a friend? Trying to blow her up and instead you kill her best friend and level her home. You screwed that one up royally.*

SK reigned in her temper and ignored the voice's taunts. She took one of the mini cameras from her purse and planted it in the trophy room. She set activation to whenever the door opened. She wanted to see Jimmy-boy in this room when he found out one of his trophies was missing.

She switched the light off, stepped out of the Copy Cat's private sanctum, closed, and locked the door. She planted another mini camera in the bedroom and gave each room a quick but through inspection to make sure nothing of her own self was left behind. She left the apartment and took the stairs down to the eighth floor to her apartment. She set up the equipment to receive any feed from the mini cams and got ready to leave. She needed to make the trip to the storage shed and she wanted to arrive shortly after the office closed. She didn't know how long it would be before she would be returning to the storage facility. She had a lot to do tomorrow before she left LA, and she still needed to make a final plan for the Copy Cat. If Rainey didn't cooperate, and the cops continued to walk around with their fingers up their asses, after she was practically giving them Jimmy-boy on a platter, she'd have to deal with him herself.

DC Britt
Saturday - Quantico

Raney dialed the number and waited. It was almost six PM in California and almost nine PM back at Quantico, but she was sure DC would still be sitting at his desk in his office.

"DC Britt."

"Evening DC. Sorry for it taking some time to get back to you. I see you're working late as usual," Rainey greeted her ex-boss.

DC skipped the niceties, "You finish up that consult, yet? I hope you are going to tell me you are preparing to fly out and join the professor in Peru."

"DC I am not flying out to Peru just yet. I called because I have some important intelligence to pass on to you. Is your computer on?"

"Yes."

"I am sending you two emails. Open and read them then call me back. I'll answer your call." Rainey closed the cell phone breaking the phone connection. She figured she had about three minutes max before her phone rang.

The phone rang within two. "Ms. Walker, I am going to have a warrant signed for your immediate arrest for obstruction," DC bellowed into Rainey's ear.

Rainey waited giving DC time to blow off steam.

"Why didn't you say anything about SK trying to make contact with you through your message service? I could have put a tap on the phone lines. The LAPD task force should have had this information. It is credible and shows they are dealing with two serial killers not just the Copy Cat. Damn it Rainey, where are you?"

"DC you just told me you are going to swear out a warrant and have me arrested. Do you really think I'm going to help you out and tell you where I am? I'm giving what information I have to you. You can deal with the LAPD, I'm not going to." You know how I feel about multi-jurisdictional law enforcement investigations and all the BS. I'm not going to be lied to or used again. Not even by you DC!"

"Okay. Okay. I was just taken by surprise. I'm not going to have you arrested. Okay?"

Rainey grinned at DC's attempt to mollify her.

"You have access to the complete Copy Cat reports. What kind of trophies is the killer taking from his victims?" Rainey waited as the silence lengthened.

"You know I can't discuss an ongoing investigation with you Rainey. You are a civilian."

Rainey expected that response. "Well then I have done my civic duty and we have nothing more to say, DC."

"Now hold on a minute, Rainey. It's clear to me that SK is trying to get you to LA. You and I know why. What I don't understand is what she's doing playing games with this Copy Cat killer. I think she knows who he is, but I don't think he knows who she is or wouldn't recognize her even if he saw her."

"I think she's using what she knows about him to get me involved in the investigation in LA. It's the only way she figures I'll go to California. I'm fairly certain she knows I am not with the FBI anymore."

"If she knows all that, then why hasn't she come after you during this last year? Seems to me it would be much simpler," DC mused.

"I've been thinking about that, too. I don't know. Only SK and her twisted mind knows, but I think she wants to kill the Six-of-Ten victim with me involved in some way, or maybe she just wants to know where I am so she doesn't have to be looking over her shoulder? She had all her target victims identified in Arizona and then she was forced to leave Arizona. She blames me for that. And let's not forget that she's probably undergone plastic surgery again and killed that doctor in San Diego."

"You may have something there. SK feels she is on a justifiable mission of revenge. Her motives are different than the Copy Cat killer. I just can't see them working a killing spree together. But then the minds of these psychotics are hard to understand, and they are almost always unpredictable when they feel pressured or trapped." DC replied.

"If anything else comes up I promise to call you. And be sure to tell the LAPD that I am presently engaged, under a business contract, and am not free to hire for consulting on their investigation. My primary interest is in SK, and will be until she is either caught or killed, and I am not particular which occurs."

"By the way, have you heard anymore from the ex-Captain Jonah Daniels?"

"Why are you asking, DC?"

"He has this private investigations business called Echo and about a week or so ago he and his partners went off the radar," DC replied.

"You keeping tabs on him like you have been me? Or do you have something else you want to ask?" Rainey's tone was sharp and she spit out the words to let DC know he was getting close to the line again.

"I had an unconfirmed report that he and his partners are somewhere in California. I thought that you also might be somewhere in California, maybe with this Echo and the ex-captain, but since you hate him and you got off a plane in Arizona with no record of taking any flights out of Arizona, you should be in Arizona. Now the thing is, Arizona and California are next door neighbors and there is just a slim possibility that you connected with him. I was just thinking of that possibility."

"DC I think you spend too much time daydreaming in that office of yours," Rainey shot back at her old boss.

"If you say so, Rainey."

"Ah... just one other thing," DC continued. "If this report is true about those Muslim communities moving all the families meeting SK's target profile out of California, then who will SK be stalking? Why is she still hanging around when she can go any-where? Nobody knows what she looks like, and she's a master at getting very good false documents. So why is she hanging around in LA and playing games with this Copy Cat killer?'

"Ah, DC, if the head of the FBI Profilers Division doesn't have any answers to that, then this ex-FBI agent can't be expected to know the answers either. If I happen to run into her, I'll be sure to ask her. I gotta run, DC. Some people are expecting me for a late dinner."

"Stay in touch, Rainey. I'll call LAPD for you and also the Phoenix PD."

Rainey grinned as she closed the cover of her cell phone. DC wasn't anybody's fool. He wasn't sure what she and Echo were up to, but he'd play along as long as she kept him in the loop. If push came to shove, he'd stand up for her. As for Jonah and Echo, she wasn't so sure.

Lieutenant Robert Jerald
Saturday late afternoon

Lieutenant Robert Jerald was a veteran Phoenix police officer and headed up the high profile crimes unit and tactical response unit. He did eight years in the military and had been a Navy Seal. The men and women who worked under his command respected him and appreciated the interest he took in each officer and their family. He was a big man, tall and well muscled with broad shoulders and narrow hips. He sat at the airport lounge bar sipping a beer. He looked relaxed, wearing tan Dockers, a brown polo shirt, and loafers. To the casual observer, he looked like any other guy waiting on his flight to be called.

The political fall-out of the SK murder investigation and escape were dumped at his door. The old axiom that 'Shit Rolls Down Hill' applied with Lieutenant Jerald. He was fortunate to have kept his lieutenant bars when the dust settled after the SK Task Force failed to capture SK. He took it in stride, and carried the weight of the personal guilt he assigned to himself. He refused to let the Phoenix case go cold after a year, though he knew he would never get promoted again. Three civilian victims slaughtered and mutilated and two veteran officers killed. Today, the killer was out there somewhere and Bob Jerald was not going to stop until the killer was put down.

Jonah sat down on the bar stool next to him. "Sorry to keep you waiting, Bob. How about we blow this place and find somewhere quiet so we can grab a bite to eat. I could use some lunch if I'm going to join you and have a beer, too."

Bob Jerald shook the hand Jonah extended. "I've cancelled my flight and decided I'd wait on rescheduling until after we talk. I have this gut feeling things are starting to happen and SK is in the middle of it."

Bob shoved his beer forward and dropped a $5.00 bill on the counter. Both men stood and headed out of the bar and airport. They took a tram to the parking lot where Jonah had left his rental car. After unlocking the doors the two men got in the front seats with Jonah proposing they go to a Mexican restaurant about three miles from the airport. Bob nodded and waited to talk until Jonah managed to negotiate through the traffic mess and clear the airport grounds heading South on one of LA's city streets.

When they got to the restaurant Bob said, "I know something is happening. We were supposed to meet in the morning, then early afternoon, then at your command center you wanted to show off, and now here we are in the late afternoon sitting in a Mexican restaurant in south LA. I'll listen and you talk, Jonah."

They both ordered draft beer. The chile relleanos, rice, pinto beans and flour tortillas were served with a huge basket of fried corn tortilla chips and tangy hot salsa. Bob began to eat.

"No fair. You get to eat and I get to smell this food and watch you eat. How about we both eat, and then we do the talk and listen?" Jonah didn't wait for Bob to reply. Instead he filled his fork with the hot Mexican food and didn't stop after the first forkful until he had cleaned his plate using a flour tortilla to sop up anything left.

"Do you know how I can always tell when things seem to be moving in the right direction with my officers in both units? Their appetites become voracious. So tell me some good news Jonah. I haven't had any good news in a year." *God I hope this isn't going to be a repeat of dribbling information in bits and pieces and me left to wonder if what I get is the straight stuff.*

Jonah seemed to sense Bob Jerald's reserve and tried to set him at ease. "Bob, the man sitting across from you is not the arrogant and bull-headed Captain Daniels loyal-to-the-government-above-all-else man you knew in Arizona. I'm retired. I screwed up and people suffered. I have to live with that. The man sitting across from you is Jonah Daniels, and my business is Echo, Private Investigations. Echo's number one objective right now is finding SK. I will spend the rest of my life, if need be, finding and bringing to justice, alive or dead, the woman we all know as Scarf Killer. No bullshit from me. No competing interests or agency politics, Bob. My business associates agree with me."

Bob sat back in his chair and seemed to visibly relax. "Okay, Jonah. You've got the floor. I'll listen." Listening was one of the his best skills.

Bob's eyes gleamed several times as Jonah talked. Jonah took a folder out of his briefcase and slid it across to Bob. "One of my partners prepared a briefing report and there are copies of the message board communications and the messages Rainey's service sent to her."

"Can't tell you enough how grateful I am that you didn't hold out on me. I'm surprised that Rainey is working with you and Echo. Even more surprised that she's willing to include me in this information sharing. She refused to see me after Sara was killed. I thought at first it was the shock of me being the one to break the news to her. I went back East to the memorial service and tried to talk to her then, but she looked right through me. The Department sent her a card and the Chief awarded her a letter of commendation, for all her help to the SK Task Force, but we never heard anything from her."

"Don't get your hopes up, Bob. She still dislikes me as much as she always has after I screwed up so badly. She's got no desire to work with operational law enforcement. She still takes a few forensic anthropology consults when an agency is looking for an ID, but that has been the extent of her law enforcement involvement this past year."

"Then it's SK that is motivating her to work with us?" Bob asked.

Jonah looked at Bob and Bob saw the traces of regret in Jonah's eyes. "If this operation was just about the Copy Cat killer she wouldn't give any of us the time of day. She is fixated on taking SK down anyway she can."

"For a time, back in Phoenix, I thought there might be something beyond the case between you and Rainey."

"There was plenty of interest on my part, but after I lied to her, it killed any feelings she might have had for me. I destroyed her trust, and she regards me as a man lacking in integrity and morals. I've learned, or am trying to learn, to live with it. I can't say for sure but I think she may be interested in a professor. She's going on one of those archeological digs with him and a group this summer. I did some checking and she's been out to dinner with him several times. I don't know if there is anything serious on her part, but what I learned is he is plenty interested in her."

Bob looked at Jonah and didn't respond. There wasn't much he felt he could say.

Jonah took the bill from the waitress when she brought it. "Can I give you a ride to the LAPD?"

"Yes. I'm going to try and get myself back on the task force, call my boss, and see if I can get my hotel room back. Hopefully the TF commander will requisition me another *guest* car to use. If not, I'll be calling Avis to rent one."

Jonah took a business card out of his briefcase and handed it to the lieutenant. "One of the Echo partners is going to be nosing around here in LA. He'll be looking for SK or the Copy Cat. Now that they're linked, Echo has an interest in both serial killers. Just call that number if you get in some kind of bind, want to share intel, or just want a friendly face to share a meal with. Drew is an unusual man. Very skilled and extremely lethal. If you are in a tight spot, he's the man to have at your back. He speaks six languages and has a PhD. Ex-military and no slouch. I call him the gentle giant behind his back. He'll ID himself to you with a hard cover card like the one I just gave you."

"And what will you, Rainey and the rest of the Echo team be doing, or should I ask?"

"Seriously?"

"Yes, Jonah, seriously."

"Rainey is finishing up a consulting job and expects to leave for Peru in a few weeks time. Right now she's just passing on information. She delayed her departure. The Echo partners and I will be doing the same thing you'll be doing, Bob. We'll be tracking down SK." Both men stood, tipped the waitress, and left the restaurant. Bob was anxious to get to the LAPD and call his boss.

Copy Cat

Saturday afternoon

James arrived at the Japanese Tea Garden five minutes early. He parked in one of the visitor parking spaces and waited. When a large minivan parked two lanes ahead of him and he counted three adults and six children pile out, he got out of the Bentley and quickly covered the space between him and the large talkative family. He stayed behind them just enough so they didn't feel uncomfortable, but anyone looking at this group might think he was a part of it.

He bought his admission ticket and hurried to catch up with the family. First thing, the kids did was beg and plead for the parents, he supposed, to buy them junk so they could get sick and most likely puke their guts. Kids were something James had little experience with. He found them to be annoying, loud and whiney. Why people bothered to have them, James had never understood. The father probably had some blue-collar job that barely paid the rent and bought food for that pack of brats and here he was spending his hard earned cash on junk for those unappreciative little blood suckers.

James looked at what he assumed was the wife. Maybe she had been pretty once, but having six kids had wrecked her figure. James shuddered, imagining lying in bed next to her rolls of fat, dry skin, and washed out scraggly hair.

This train of thought is bringing down my high. James found the same bench SK had told him to sit on and wait for her the first time when she had failed to show up. The bench was in the shade of a large tree. He sat down and watched the entrance and exit gate and the intersection where the foot paths splintered off. *This is the perfect place for SK to notice me and for me to spot a woman by herself looking for someone.* James glanced at his wrist watch. *Any minute and she should walk in alone and spot me sitting under the tree.* James was so excited his hands were trembling.

At five o'clock James was still sitting on the bench. His eyes had a murderous look. People walking by started to give him a friendly greeting, but when they saw his face, they quickened their steps and hurried past the angry man they heard softly muttering vile curse words.

"That bitch. Whore! Piece of slime shit! She's made a fool of me again. This time I don't forgive and forget. I'll kill her if it's the last act I commit. I'll tear her skin from her face while she screams in agony. I'll cut the joints from her hands one at a time while she suffers knowing that a foot or an arm or an eye could be next and I'll keep her alive. Yes. I'll keep her alive for days and torture her till she begs me to kill her, but I won't. I'll give her transfusions just to keep her alive a few more days."

The rage was mounting and James' ears felt as if they would explode. He had only been denied something once in his entire life. His hatred for his father denying him the animals he needed to assuage his blood lust burned deep inside of him. Now there was SK. She had denied him and made a fool of him twice.

He was sweating profusely now, and his body shook all over. The sweat poured into his eyes and blinded him temporarily. From what seemed a great distance, James heard a voice speaking, but he could not make out the words. James grabbed a corner of his shirt and wiped his eyes.

There was a man standing in front of him. *What is he saying?* James was in a panic.

"Hey mister, are you okay? Do you need a doctor? Can you hear me?"

Gradually his eyes began to focus and James realized the man standing in front of him was a hired security officer. People passing by had seen James and grew concerned at his strange behavior and had reported it to the admissions employee.

SK caused this, he screamed inside his head. *She brought this unwanted attention to me.* James struggled to reign in his rage.

Gradually he made out what the security officer was saying.

"I'm sorry officer. I didn't mean to frighten anyone. I have these spells now and then and I have medication that controls them. I must have forgotten to take my medicine today. But the symptoms run their course and I'm feeling better. Thank you for your concern."

The officer handed James a bottle of water. A lady who was standing in a small crowd that had gathered handed him a white hankie. James thanked them profusely and gave them his most charming smile. He could see the tension disappearing from the onlookers and they began to drift away.

"You sure you're going to be okay? I can call for some medical help."

"No. I'm much better thank you. I do think that I had better go on home today and come back to enjoy the gardens on another day." His voice had slowly recovered and he had stopped shaking.

The security officer looked relieved that he would not have to make a report. He didn't even bother to ask James for some identification. "Do you need me to help you to your car? You can drive okay now?"

James stood and showed the officer that he was well on the road to recovering from his 'minor episode.' James thanked the officer again and purposefully walked towards the exit gate. He walked through it and made it to his car. When he climbed inside, he started the engine and blasted the radio. James put his head down on the steering wheel and screamed his rage.

Undercover

Saturday evening

The drive from LA back to Brantlie was without incident and Rainey actually relaxed during the drive. Just knowing Rand was not too far behind her in the Command Center RV was comforting. About two miles from the city limits, Rainey pulled to the side of the road and waited for Rand to catch up. When he pulled up behind her, she got out of the car and walked back to the passenger side of the RV.

"I wanted you to know that I'll be having dinner in tonight. Tomorrow morning Ibrahim and another Muslim will be taking me to the Sultana Books & More department store. I'll be introduced and begin my first day of work as a sales clerk. Some of the brothers in the community are on high alert, so any stranger will be looked at closely. When you tail me keep a distance. Not all the men will be aware of what we are doing. The Muslim men are pretty sharp and they don't like men looking at what they consider their sisters. That means staring or watching. Most of them won't know who you are, so don't get into trouble by being too obvious. And Muslim women don't chit-chat casually with men, not even with Muslim men.

"Thanks for the refresher, Rainey. Jonah, Drew, and I had a discussion about Muslim etiquette so I'll try not to call attention to myself or to you." Rand handed her what looked like a small hearing aid. "Put this in your ear tomorrow and I'll be able to hear what is being said, so you can talk to me directly. It is very sensitive. Rand showed her a tiny button. Just press this before you put it in your ear."

Rainey put the piece of equipment in a side pocket in her purse.

"I forgot to tell all of you that there is a park in the center of town with running trails. I don't think I'm up to running in the abeya, veil, and scarf, but if I go to the park I'll take a lunch and a book, so it will look like I am enjoying myself reading and relaxing in the park. SK runs every day, and if she is coming to Brantlie to stalk Amira, there is a chance I might spot her on one of her runs."

"That's important to know. I'll pass it on to Jonah and Drew. Jonah called and said he's been delayed. I'll tell him to call you later."

"You be careful, Rand. Don't underestimate SK. She can spot a cop or military better than most people. See ya."

"Watch your back," Rand replied as Rainey closed the Command Center door behind her.

Rainey turned right onto Catalina Street and noticed two flatbed trucks parked in front of Ibrahim and Jamilah's house. There were at least a dozen vehicles and pickup trucks lined up along the street on both sides. Rainey could see in the last of daylight many Muslim men busy working on erecting a chain link fence around Ibrahim's property.

How did he get the construction materials and city permits to do this immediately? Rainey wondered as she slowed down to look for a place to park along the street. Rainey pulled into the only empty space across from the house, got out, and locked the car. She walked across the street to a group of men standing with Ibrahim near his front porch.

"Salaams." Rainey said and her smile included everyone in the group. The men nodded their heads and moved away a short distance from Rainey and Ibrahim. "It looks like you have had a busy day?"

Ibrahim nodded and cleared his throat. "Last night we had a discussion and we felt it would be best to enclose the property. There will be a card gate key when we finish the work tomorrow and also an alarm. When you use the key you will remember to push the alarm off first."

"Yes, of course I will remember. Thank you for telling me." When Ibrahim said *we,* Rainey knew he meant the group of imams.

"We have taken a few other precautions for your safety and everyone staying in the bungalows on my property."

Rainey waited until Ibrahim was ready to continue. When he saw that Rainey did not have any comment he continued, "Two brothers have moved into each of the bungalows that are on either side of the one you are staying in. They will watch at night to be sure you are not disturbed."

These men are well-intentioned but are no match for SK. They could be placing themselves in real danger, Rainey thought. Instead of saying this she asked, "Have they had any kind of military or law enforcement training, Ibrahim?"

"Yes. The four volunteers that were selected have military experience. Two are reservists. They don't intend to fire weapons, but only to watch and alert the police at any sign of a problem. They will make sure your bungalow will not be entered by anyone while you are at work or away from it. Do these precautions seem reasonable? We hope they are approved. There was no time to set up a meeting with you first. We only just thought of this last night after it was too late to disturb you."

"The arrangements you have made and all the trouble you have gone through are appreciated."

"Good. We are not police type people, so we relied on the young men who call themselves your 'look-outs'. Ibrahim smiled at the self-designation.

Rainey kept a serious face and asked Ibrahim to thank everyone for her. The men were gathering their tools and getting readying to leave. It would soon be prayer time.

Ibrahim asked for Rainey's car keys. "One of the brothers will move your car to the front of the bungalow later and will knock at the door to give you the keys. Did you have your evening meal?"

Rainey was exhausted and begged off dinner. Ibrahim did not try to dissuade her. He looked tired, too. It had been a busy day. Rainey was almost certain if SK was in California and was reading Muslim newspapers, she would be showing up in Brantlie very soon. Maybe even as soon as tomorrow.

Copy Cat

Saturday evening

James looked at his face in the rear view mirror and then down at his sweat stained and wrinkled clothing. His demeanor looked calm but the rage was still in his eyes. The blood lust was throbbing and James knew how he would assuage it. He muttered to himself, "I'll find you bitch, and when I do you'll beg me for mercy."

James drove to Christopher's apartment complex and parked the Bentley. Tonight would be the final Copy Cat kill. He would be taking care of family business and spending time hunting down and destroying SK. He needed to get cleaned up before he did anything else. It was after six PM and the night security officer had come on duty. The guy waved at the Bentley's heavily tinted windows. Everyone working at the complex knew the Bentley. In the apartment James walked to the master bedroom, took off the wig and soiled clothing, and headed for the bathroom. After a cold five minute shower, he picked up the phone and dialed.

"Hallo, Dee-Dee speaking."

"Dee-Dee, darling. I just got back to my hotel room from the office." He waited for the slut to stop talking. "I know, but this merger called for an all day round of meetings and we got things wrapped up. I got back to my hotel room and there was no one to celebrate with. I didn't want to hang around with those old coots.

I sat down on the edge of my bed and thought, Christopher, why not call Dee-Dee and surprise her. I just hated to tear myself away last night and I haven't thought of anything all day except you. I was thinking about cancelling my flight and staying over a few more days. I've certainly earned some down time and I'd like to see more of you. I know it is really short notice, but I hate to think about ordering a hotel dinner and eating in my room alone. I thought I'd take the chance and call you and see if you were free tonight. I'll understand after I left you so abruptly last night, if you say no." James made a big production of letting out a big sigh and said softly, "Are you free tonight, Dee-Dee?"

"Christopher aren't you ever so sweet. Wanting to cancel your flight so we can spend some time together and asking me to celebrate with you. That is just too precious. I'd love to have dinner with you. Where shall we go? Oh, I know. Why don't you surprise me when you get here."

"I'd love to surprise you, Dee-Dee, darling, but I was thinking maybe we could eat in. I have so little time and just hate to think about sharing you with waiters and doormen, and a bunch of people I don't know all staring at you. You are so beautiful Dee-Dee." James gave a low sexy growl and then a soft laugh. He could just see the idiot swooning and simpering.

"Christopher that is a lovely idea. I'll call for room service and have everything ready for when you get here." Dee-Dee's voice had dropped as she purred her response to him.

"Give me about an hour. I need to shower and change. When I get to the lobby I'll call so you can unlock your door. You're keeping it locked like I cautioned you?"

"Oh absolutely, Christopher. You are such a sweetie and so thoughtful. See you at seven, bye."

James bared his teeth in a semblance of a grin. "She'll be ready and waiting with the door unlocked. How very helpful you are Dee-Dee." The look on James' face was anything but thoughtful.

He dressed casually, but tastefully. He opened the bureau drawer and took out his murder kit. The brown leather bag was shaped much like an over-sized shaving kit. He selected a human hair wig from a second drawer and from another drawer took out a professional artists' make up kit.

Standing in front of the dresser mirror he rapidly applied makeup and adjusted the wig. The final touch was carefully putting the blue contacts in his eyes. "Good evening Christopher Carrington. Are we all ready to go play house with Dee-Dee?"

He looked at the reflection of Christopher Carrington and gave him a wolfish grin. The now blue eyes staring back at him through the colored lenses could not hide his rage. Next he clicked off the light, put the murder kit under his left arm, and strode through the apartment, going out the front door and locking it. Christopher Carrington walked to the elevator, stepped inside, and rode it down to underground garage.

He pulled the Bentley into the driveway in front of the Waldorf. The six blocks between the apartment and the hotel seemed to have taken forever. Tonight he was in a hurry and could hardly contain himself and his lust. He put the gear in park and waited as the valet hurried to his door to open it. He tossed the keys into the outstretched hand of the valet and handed him a ten spot. "You be real careful with my baby," he cautioned with his charming smile. The valet nodded taking the ten spot and waiting until Christopher had stepped around the Bentley and approached the lobby doors where the doorman was waiting.

He nodded to the doorman, handing him a twenty dollar bill as he entered and walked towards the elevators. He pressed the button and stepped into the elevator. When the door closed he let go of his control temporarily and allowed the feelings of anticipation and the lust to take over. "Almost there. Almost there, Christopher." He opened his cell phone and dialed letting the phone ring three times before hanging up. Dee-Dee just loved drama, and so did Christopher. Good old Christopher had let her think the little game of three rings and the hang up was her idea. She would be waiting in the bedroom for him. They always were.

He looked at his wrist watch, seven o'clock straight up. He walked down the hallway to Dee-Dee's apartment door. He turned the doorknob and heard the click. "Good girl," he said softly as he gently pushed the door open and closed it behind him taking care to lock the door. Christopher was ready to give Dee-Dee her big surprise.

Christopher carefully dressed and looked around the room. He felt relaxed as he surveyed his handiwork. He picked up his trophy and carefully placed it in the bag inside the murder kit. He hadn't been able to prolong the play. His blood lust boiled over and it was all over before that thing on the floor knew what had hit her. Christopher adjusted the wig and made sure his makeup wasn't smeared. Eight-thirty the dial on his watch said.

He glanced at the once lovely thing on the floor. The Post-it note was stuck to her forehead and the silken Muslim scarf covered it and her face. His last Copy Cat kill. He had decided to leave the thing naked except for the scarf.

He laughed as he surveyed his handiwork one last time. He picked up the murder kit and walked out of the bedroom and apartment making sure he closed, but didn't lock the door. Christopher stepped out of the elevator. The doorman saw him and called to the valet to get the Bentley. Christopher tipped the doorman and valet a second time. They would have no problem remembering Christopher when questioned by the police.

Christopher decided to drive to Club 21. He was near starving after his playtime performance. A large steak and a bottle of the best wine grandfather's money can buy was in order. It was celebration time, and he was feeling good.

* * *

It was almost eleven o'clock when James, driving the Bentley, approached the underground parking security station of the apartment building. The security officer recognized him as Christopher and buzzed the gate letting him through. He parked the Bentley next to the car belonging to James E. Thornton III.

He got out of the Bentley talking to himself, "Man, am I ever tired. You were a busy guy tonight, Christopher!" He retrieved the murder kit from the front passenger seat before locking the car. He took the elevator up to the tenth floor and walked the short distance to the apartment. Unlocking the door, he stepped inside and secured it. He flipped on the overhead light and continued to the master bedroom.

James walked to the bureau and in the bottom drawer lifted out the crystal jar with the liquid preservative. James took the lid off the jar and set the jar and lid on the dresser. He walked over to the bed where he had placed the murder kit on top of the bedspread, opened the kit, and took out his new prize.

Gently taking his new trophy out of the bag, he let it slide slowly down into the liquid until it was completely immersed. James put the lid back on the jar and twisted it tight. "Ah!" He held up the crystal jar admiring his latest work. The finger was long and slender with a beautifully buffed and polished red nail. "I'll get a plaque made for you soon, but first things first."

James looked at his watch. "Christopher has another busy evening tomorrow, so get moving." James carried the crystal jar into the bathroom to keep him company while he showered. After dressing in slacks and polo shirt, James decided to take his new trophy with him back to the penthouse so he could enjoy it a while longer. He'd put it with the other trophies tomorrow after he took care of the family matter.

SK

Saturday early evening

SK used her after-hours pass code to open the gate of the storage facility. She drove down to the last two buildings where the largest spaces were located, and parked in front of her unit. She unlocked and rolled up the door and switched on the light.

She got back in the SUV and drove inside, parking next to a gleaming black and silver Yamaha 650 motorcycle with two side saddle bags and a helmet with a tinted visor setting on the seat. She got out of the SUV and pulled down the shed door half way.

A large olive green foot-locker sat in one corner of the space, which SK unlocked as she sat on the floor. Opening the lid, her eyes gleamed as she found the embroidered pillow that was protecting the trophies she prized inside it. SK lifted the pillow and placed it carefully in her lap and began to pull the zipper down along the edge of the pillow.

You think you deserve to fondle your trophies, do you? The grating voice sneered at SK.

SK let go of the zipper and clapped her hands over her ears. "Shut up! Just shut up!" she screamed trying to silence the voice.

There are only five trophies inside. Only five and where are the others? It's been a year since you ran like a coward from Arizona and you have nothing to show but collateral damage and the game you're playing with the Copy Cat. He's making all the headlines while you still haven't even found Rainey Walker.

The white noise in her head blasted her and the pain shot across her eyes. SK looked down but her eyes were temporarily blinded with pain. She couldn't see the pillow and she trembled with rage.

"Leave me be. I have a plan, and very soon Rainey Walker will be where I want her and Six-of-Ten will be mine. I don't know where all the Muslim women went, but I finally found one and she will be dead and soon."

Maybe and maybe not. Maybe your friend the Copy Cat will find you first. Then what? Then you will be the victim and die a failure. Your mission compromised by the time you have wasted on a common killer. How ironic, the voice taunted her.

SK stood, and ignoring the pain and the voice, she placed the pillow in one of the saddle bags. She retrieved the crystal jar from the large handbag in the SVU and carefully wrapped it with a towel from the foot locker. SK placed the crystal jar in the saddle bag with her pillow, closed the top, and secured it.

SK took her .22, the silencer, and the carton of Black Talon ammo out of her handbag. Opening the other saddle bag, she took out the one piece driving suit, black riding boots, and gloves. She put her weapon, silencer, ammo, and a six-inch serrated knife in the empty saddle bag and secured it. SK dressed quickly and walked the Yamaha out of the storage space, rolling down the door and securing the locks afterwards. She walked the bike to the storage facility gate, entered her pass code, and walked the bike through the gates. She depressed the close button and once the gate was secured she got on the bike, started the engine, and took off.

SK got home close to ten o'clock. She thought about going to the other apartment to see if Copy Cat discovered one of his trophies was missing, but the taunting of the voice earlier reminded her she needed to stay focused on her mission. There would be time to go back and see the video at the other apartment after she had taken care of business. Time enough then to take care of Copy Cat. SK had a busy day lined up for tomorrow and needed a good night's rest.

Copy Cat

Sunday morning

Bringing his newest trophy home to the penthouse had been a mistake. He had a busy day planned for Sunday and needed to get some sleep. Instead, he kept looking at his trophy and fantasizing about the kill. He posted a last message to that bitch SK on the message board. Now he regretted letting her know how much her being a no-show a second time had bothered him. It made falling asleep difficult. He had admired SK for using that Phoenix cop and wasting him and then escaping Arizona and leaving nothing behind but a cold trail. Why he thought they could become friends eluded him. He wanted someone to share his exploits with, talk freely with. Stupid idea! He finally drifted off about three AM after setting his alarm for eight. Five hours would just have to be enough sleep.

James heard the alarm and came instantly awake. He tossed back the covers and padded to the living room where his trophy sat on the coffee table covered with a towel. He was tempted to take a quick look but resisted and instead got showered and dressed and called for breakfast.

"Good morning. Mr. Thornton in the penthouse."

"Good morning, Mr. Thornton. How may we assist you today?"

"I'd like a light breakfast sent to my room, not the usual, and send a pot of tea instead of coffee, please. I'm feeling a bit under the weather."

"We are sorry to hear you are unwell. Your order will be a priority, Sir."

James thanked the man and hung the receiver back on the land-line phone. He walked to the coffee table and picked up the crystal jar with its trophy inside and carried it to the bedroom where he placed it on the dresser. He went back to the living room after closing the bedroom door behind him and removing the temptation to gaze at his trophy.

A few minutes later the knock on his front door interrupted James. Breakfast had arrived. James signed the bill and tipped the waiter. He should have had the food delivered using the dumb-waiter to avoid contact, but he thought about that after the knock on the door. He didn't want any employees telling anyone how 'healthy' he looked today.

The dumbwaiter was an ingenious method of quickly sending meals or items long-term tenants ordered through the front desk when staff was busy. It saved time and kept the elevators from being clogged with the food and luggage carts.

James sipped his tea, but was too keyed up to eat anything. Ordering the light breakfast so he could mention to the front desk that he was not feeling well was part of the plan to give him an alibi for tonight. "I'll leave a message later with the front desk before I get ready to leave asking not to be disturbed. I've got a busy schedule after I leave from Grandfather's family dinner." A sly smile crossed his face as the blood lust urge began to roil inside him. His plan was simple. A piece of cake.

He'd leave the penthouse at six, using the stairs to the basement, exit through the back door to the alleyway, walk a few blocks and then catch a taxi to Christopher's place. He'd walk in like a guest and take the elevator to the tenth floor. After getting dressed as Christopher, he'd take the elevator to the parking garage and make sure security got a visual on Christopher driving the Bentley as he left the garage.

After taking care of family business, he'd drive to the airport, ditch the Bentley, and catch a taxi to the storage place where he'd stored the pickup and hand cart. He'd drive the pickup to Christopher's apartment and park it in one of the guest parking places. Next he'd pack the trunks, sanitize the apartment, and stage it for the cops. He'd drive the pickup back to the storage place and leave it. He'd call a taxi and get back to the penthouse getting up to his apartment the same way he left it.

James paused and poured another cup of tea and sipped it slowly while going over the details of the first part of the plan a second time. He smiled with satisfaction.

All that would be left to do was show up at the Monday morning VIP meeting and wait for the cops to show up and give me the family notification, he thought with glee. He'd take all his important papers with him, a large stash of cash, and his notebook and charger. He'd allow that old fart, the company attorney, to deal with the cops, maybe tell them he'd go with James to make an ID of his family later in the afternoon and would go to police headquarters to give a statement if the cops insisted. He'd have his secretary call a taxi to take him back to his penthouse so he could rest. Once there, he'd wait until the taxi drove off, walk a few blocks to the nearest bus stop, and lose himself in the city.

When he didn't show up at the police station, the cops would come to the penthouse apartment looking for him but wouldn't find him. They might think something horrible had happened to him because they'd find his Caddy parked in its reserved place and learn that no one at Thornton Towers had seen him.

James rubbed his hands together relishing his plan. I'll get a room at some flea bag motel and on Tuesday begin the hunt for SK. I will become a missing person. It will be a mystery as to what happened to me. I'll stay missing until I find that bitch and destroy her. Then I'll wander into some business all dirty and confused telling people I can't remember who I am. Everyone will think I was so grief stricken I just wandered off. James laughed at that thought.

When they find the Bentley abandoned at the airport they'll think Christopher took flight, but there won't be any ticket purchased for Christopher Carrington. They will find his apartment and inside my little, or should I say, Copy Cat's little surprise for them. James laughed a hideous laugh when he thought again of how he was going to stage Christopher's apartment. Let the cops taste again the bitterness of their failures!

James yawned and rubbed the back of his neck while walking back to his bedroom. He decided to take a nap. He had a lot to do tonight and into the early hours of the next morning. He set the alarm for five PM and then crawled back into bed.

Operation SK

Saturday morning

Rainey shut off the alarm at eight o'clock to start her day. Using the throw rug as her exercise mat she began a series of stretches. *I miss my daily run,* she groaned as she worked muscles that had been ignored for the last four days. After a bowl of cereal and glass of orange juice, Rainey got ready for her first day of work at the department store. *I hope they have a coffee pot somewhere in the employee break room. Hmm maybe they don't have a break room? Surely they do. Muslims eat lunch like anyone else. Stop it, Rainey. You are just nervous and are going on about nothing.* Rainey laughed at herself for her lapse into a mild spasm of new job jitters. She put on the abeya, hijab, and veil and checked herself in the mirror. She almost forgot the gloves. Rainey had checked her five-shot Chief Special before turning in the previous evening. Trying to get to the revolver from a shoulder holster would have proven too difficult, so Rainey strapped it to the ankle holster above her left ankle. Rainey opened the front door to see Ibrahim, Salim and Salim's wife, Saba standing by Ibrahim's car. They were taking her to work today to introduce her to the store owner. In the future, Saba would come by to take her to work and then bring her home afterwards. In her role as Amira, Rainey would not be driving.

"Salaams everyone," she said and they returned the greeting.

Saba handed her a cup of Starbucks coffee. "I brought it black. I think this is your preference?"

Rainey took the cup of coffee, nodded and smiled her gratitude. Rainey and Saba got into the back seat of the car and Ibrahim and Salim got in the front seats.

Ibrahim turned to Salim and said, "I see our volunteer fence workers are arriving. They should have the fence and gate completed by noon today, *insha Allah*."

He turned in the seat and said to Rainey, "Saba will give you a gate key when she picks you up at the store about five o'clock."

Rainey opened her handbag and took out a photograph. She handed the photograph to Ibrahim. "This man works with the investigators who are hunting SK. He will be in the community. The brothers working security may see him at the mosque, the store, and other places. Please ask them to greet him as though he were a brother in your community. He will be watching me and watching for SK. His name is Rand. If I need to meet with the investigators at night he may show up here to get me or I may drive to a location to meet him and the other investigator. The other investigator will not make himself visible or known in the community." Both Ibrahim and Salim nodded they understood.

"Rainey, do you think this killer will come to our community soon?"

"I don't know, Salim. I'm expecting that she is already in the region, if not in this community already. It has been over a year now since she fled Arizona, and she must be frustrated at not being able to locate a Muslim woman fitting the victim profile. Now that Amira has surfaced, she may have read about her in the newspaper and will come after her here, but I don't know how long she'll stalk Amira before she decides to strike."

"You are very brave to do this," Saba said softly.

"I'm not brave, I'm scared, Saba. But if we, the community, and the other investigators don't try to stop her here, she will move on to another place, and we won't know where until she kills again. We have to try and stop that from happening."

The car fell silent for the remainder of the trip, each person lost in thought. The gravity of all but inviting the killer to come to their community was not lost on them, nor was the fact that the local police had yet to be informed.

Khaled Eldawy was all smiles as he greeted Rainey and his Muslim friends accompanying her into his office. Rainey towered over her new employer. He was dressed impeccably in a dark blue suit, crisp white shirt and red and blue striped tie. The shine on his black shoes would have passed any police inspection.

He looks a complete opposite of Salim and Ibrahim, Rainey thought. Khaled's short graying hair was combed back and he had used a generous amount of gel. His beard and mustache were neatly trimmed. In contrast, Ibrahim and Salim's beards were long and well, bushy. Their hair was much longer and tied back, and their clothing was casual and toned down.

"As Salaam 'Alaykum. Welcome." Khaled hurried to move chairs closer to his desk. "Please sit down and we will have some tea."

From long experience with Muslims, Rainey knew that the courtesies were observed before any business was discussed. She relaxed and looked around at the office while Khaled busied himself pouring tea for everyone. The office was as neat as Khaled's appearance. *How can anyone work in such an orderly place? If I worked in here, it'd be a mess in no time!*

Saba sat next to her husband, leaned towards him and whispered in his ear. He nodded and patted her arm. Saba stood up and excused herself before leaving the room and shutting the office door quietly behind her.

"My wife gives her apologies. She has some errands to take care of. She will return this afternoon to drive you back to Ibrahim's place, Rainey."

Rainey did not find Saba's leaving the meeting unusual. She would have been uncomfortable sitting with the men though she was probably curious about the plans they would be discussing. *She'll probably be filled in by her husband before bedtime,* Rainey thought. After everyone had taken a few sips of tea, Khaled picked up a paper from the top of the desk and handed it to Rainey.

"This is the employment application for Amira. We will keep it in our files until you no longer need to be here at the store. I am at the store each day, but if I must leave for any reason, my eldest son, Yusuf, will be in the store to assist you. I will introduce you once we finish with business here."

Rainey nodded, looked over the application, and handed it back to Khaled.

Ibrahim took the photo of Rand from his pocket and handed it to Khaled. "Could you make some copies of this photo for brother Salim and me? The man's name is Rand and he is an investigator who will be in our community and watching Amira. Salim will take copies to the masjid to give to our security."

Khaled took the photo and walked to the door. He opened it and stuck his head out speaking in Arabic to someone who came to the door and took the photograph. "Sister A'aminah will make the copies and bring them to me shortly."

Khaled returned to his chair behind his neat and orderly desk. He turned to Rainey once again and this time he addressed her as Amira and spoke in Arabic.

All three men smiled when they heard her answer in Arabic, "I am glad I will be working in the English language book section. My Arabic is adequate, but my knowledge of the Middle Eastern items I saw as we walked though the store is limited. I would not want to embarrass my Uncle Ibrahim by appearing to your customers to be an ignorant immigrant." The three men smiled, acknowledging Rainey's joke.

"What is your plan if this killer comes into the store?" Khaled asked, switching to English for Rainey's comfort.

"The less your employees know, the better it will be for this operation and for them. If you have not told them I am a plant, let's keep this fact among ourselves. If SK comes into the store and I identify her, I will keep this to myself and take no action inside the store. I am wearing a device which allows me voice contact with Rand, who will be close by. We will allow SK to leave the store so no one inside will get harmed. She is very dangerous and I don't know what she would do if she felt trapped."

"I have not told the employees anything about you. The women would be very nervous if I did. I should tell my son Yusuf in case you need assistance, though, because as you said, this killer is unpredictable."

"That would be okay. I also want you to know I am armed. I have a weapon on my body. I am trained and qualified with this weapon. I would only use it if necessary to save a life."

Khaled and the two other men in the room looked at Rainey. Their expressions were serious and they were silent. Rainey waited. The men were thinking or praying or both.

"My son Yusuf works for an armed security company. He donates time at our masjid on his days off as we have needed this security since 9/11. In the fall he will return to classes. He is working part time for me this summer and he also is armed, but with a Glock pistol. He is qualified and is very careful. He does not excite easily."

Not too sure how I feel about someone I don't know carrying, Rainey thought as she listened to Khaled.

Ibrahim, very sensitive to the body language of people, noticed Rainey's tension as she tugged on the edges of her scarf. "Is there a problem with Yusuf being armed? We expected you to be armed. We thought you would expect us to have taken some steps also?"

Rainey shook her head slightly. "No, there isn't a problem. I am glad you informed me. Please let him know that the plan is not to take any kind of action inside the store if I identify her." The three men nodded agreement.

"I think this concludes our meeting. Sister A'aminah should have copies of the photo ready by now. If you make a sale, Amira, you will have the buyer go to a check-out station. You do not have to handle the checkout. Your work will be to give customer assistance or tell them about any book they ask for. We have a form you can give a customer if we do not have a book in stock or carry a book they want. You will also put new books we have received on the shelves, but I will be sure there are not too many new books. We do not want to keep you too busy. You will need time to wander throughout the store so you will be able to become familiar with the store as well as have the opportunity to look at customers."

"Excellent. With the article in the newspaper yesterday I am expecting SK to be close, if not already in the community making her plan to stalk me. I'd like to be able to identify her without giving her the opportunity to harm anyone she thinks is hindering her from getting to me."

Rainey and the three men stood when they heard the knock on the office door. Khaled walked to the door as it opened, and a woman wearing hijab scarf and abeya but no face veil or gloves handed him a stack of papers.

"Salaams and thank you sister A'aminah. I am pleased to introduce you to Brother Ibrahim's niece, Sister Amira. Please speak in English so our sister can become more familiar with hearing and speaking the language of her new adopted country."

The smiling woman turned her smile on Rainey. "As Salaam'Alaykum, Sister Amira. Welcome to our community and to our country. You will find things very different here, but do not be concerned. I am here to help you. All the sisters will help you. Soon enough you will be feeling like part of the community."

Rainey returned salaams and then followed A'aminah from the office to begin her new job as sales clerk.

The morning passed slowly for Rainey. Patience, she silently scolded herself. SK will need time to prepare and set up before she starts stalking Amira.

Rainey heard Rand's voice in her right ear. "Rainey, DC is hopping mad. He's called Jonah three times. Wouldn't tell him anything. The man hates Jonah. Said he had an urgent need to talk to you. Said you had given your word not to turn off your phone and would stay in contact."

Rainey groaned. She had turned off her cell phone for the meeting and forgotten to turn it on to vibrate for incoming calls. Rainey stooped over and picked up a book while speaking quickly to Rand, "I'll call him. Nothing is happening here. I'll talk to you after speaking to DC."

Rainey asked A'aminah to be excused to go to the restroom. Wearing the abeya, she could not easily access her phone in public.

Rainey entered the women employees' restroom and locked the door. This was the only private room in the building other than Khaled's office. She reached inside the abeya to the pocket in her skirt and pulled out her cell phone. There were missed calls from DC and Jonah.

Rainey speed dialed DC. "Where in the Sam Hill have you been, Walker? I have been trying to reach you for two hours!" Rainey could picture DC sitting ramrod straight in his chair behind that massive desk and tightly gripping a number two pencil as he bellowed into the speakerphone.

She replied calmly, "At a meeting, and I am sorry for forgetting to turn the phone back on."

DC's voice raised thirty decibels, "Rainey, I want to know where you are, now, stop stalling. Your old friend Jonah told me he didn't know but the man is a liar. He knows and if I find him, I will arrest him and have him prosecuted. Him and that Echo team of his."

Rainey's tone of voice was clipped and measured, "I was told you had something urgent to tell me?" Rainey waited until she heard DC's breathing quiet and his voice return to normal. Her ex-boss definitely had a temper.

"All hell is breaking loose and now I've got the head of the LAPD task force calling my boss complaining about obstruction and withholding information, and that cop from Phoenix who was on the task force is in one of their interrogation rooms being grilled. His chief in Phoenix is on my case, wanting to know what I'm holding back, and everyone and his uncle is looking for you."

Rainey let DC wind down without interrupting him. He seemed to pause so she started to speak, "Lieutenant Jerald is being interrogated? Is he under arrest? What for?"

DC didn't answer Rainey's questions. Instead he said, "I sent an agent to babysit your message service and another message came in for you this morning. Agent Brantley also identified another message on that message board late last night. This one was from the Copy Cat and SK hasn't replied to it. I now know why, after hearing the message SK left for you."

Rainey had a feeling of dread. SK was intent on trying to make contact with her. Rainey knew she would never give up, not as long as Rainey was breathing and in this world. Rainey wanted contact with SK too, but as Amira.

Rainey knew DC would get around to the lieutenant when he was ready, so she said instead, "Why not start with SK's message and then you can tell me the message the Copy Cat left for SK?"

"The message was brief, but just long enough to trace it to LA. In fact, it came from a restaurant just three blocks from police headquarters. The waitress on shift is being interrogated and LAPD is tracking down the customers in the restaurant at the time of the phone call."

This is getting stranger by the minute, Rainey thought as she continued to listen to DC's story.

"Seems a tall, thin man wearing wire-rimmed glasses and a charcoal grey business suit asked a waitress if he could use the phone. He was carrying a medium sized box that was wrapped in brown paper. The man said the box was a present for his wife. He told the waitress his cell phone died and some vandals had cut the tires on his car. He wanted to call for a tow truck and then call his wife to come and pick him up. The waitress was obliging, especially when this man plunked down a twenty dollar bill to thank her. After he made his calls the waitress noticed the man place the box on the stool beside him. The word *Fragile* was printed in large letters on the side of the box. He ordered a cup of coffee but didn't drink it. He was supposed to have been waiting for his wife. The waitress got busy and didn't notice anything until she saw him going out the door without the package. She hurried after him but when she got outside, she didn't see him anyplace. She figured his wife must have come for him and he would be back as soon as he realized he had left the present on the stool. She later told the cops that the man was almost feminine in the way he looked and walked."

"I hate to interrupt DC, but I think you got off track. You were going to tell me about the phone message from SK?"

"I was trying to answer your question about Lieutenant Jerald because it ties in with SK's message to you and I think to the Copy Cat's message. That package is why the lieutenant is being interrogated and why I am taking a lot of heat."

"Sorry. Just go ahead and I'll listen without interrupting you again."

"The message to you said, "I left you a present at the LAPD with your old friend from Phoenix PD. I have some business to attend to. When I return to LA I'll call you. SK." This time she used the letters S and K."

"The package that was left at the restaurant…."

"Yes, that package. It was addressed to Lieutenant Jerald, Phoenix PD in care of the LAPD Copy Cat Task Force. After the bomb squad made sure it was not an explosive device the package was taken to the task force headquarters. The task force commander had Lieutenant Jerald rousted from his motel room, cuffed, and taken to headquarters for interrogation. The task force commander is fuming."

This is reading like some kind of movie script. SK loves to manipulate and create drama, Rainey thought but asked, "What was inside the package?"

"I'm getting to that. First let me tell you about the Copy Cat's message to Es Que."

"Okay." Rainey said and waited.

"I think a budding courtship is over. The message was brief and to the point. It said, "Es Que. You bitch. I'll find you! Si! Si!""

Rainey thought, *Would she have done something that outrageous?* The implications of SK's message to her and Copy Cat's angry message to SK left on the message board hit Rainey.

"Are you telling me SK took something personal from the Copy Cat and sent it to the LAPD Task Force? My god, she knows where he lives. She found his trophies and sent one in that package to Lieutenant Jerald, didn't she? That is creepy. It's disturbing. What kind of game is she playing?"

"It gets worse, Rainey."

"Worse?" Rainey's voice cracked.

"When the package was opened there was a crystal jar and inside it was the finger of what the task force commander, Captain Jenkins, believes will be identified as belonging to the Copy Cat's Victim 3. They'll confirm this once forensics is through testing."

"The Copy Cat must be in a rage right now."

"I haven't finished, Rainey. There was a photograph taken of a dark room, and in it was a display case with soft lighting shining down on padded shelves with 14 more jars on the shelves. The jars look like the one SK sent to the task force. There were objects in the jars but to the naked eye, Jenkins said they couldn't make out what was in the jars. Their experts will be working with enlarging the photo to see if they can identify what's inside."

"They must all be thinking there are other fingers of victims or possibly different body parts in the jars. Fourteen other jars? That means the Copy Cat has victims unknown to the LAPD." The enormity of this new information was staggering.

"It gets worse, Rainey."

"DC, how can it get any worse?"

"There was a letter with the package and the envelope had your name printed on it."

There was a knock on the restroom door and Rainey heard Sister A'aminah ask, "Sister Amira are you okay? Brother Yusuf and I are worried as you have been in there so long. Are you feeling sick?"

"DC I'll call you back in a few minutes."

Rainey closed the phone cover and answered A'aminah, "I am okay, A'aminah. I think I am just nervous about my first day at work and my lunch does not want to stay put. I will be out in a few minutes."

"If you need me, I will be waiting outside. Perhaps you might want to have a short day today and go home and rest. I can ask Brother Khaled. I am sure it would be fine with him if you left a little early."

"I am feeling better. I will be okay. Thank you for your kindness, sister. I will be back in the book section in a few minutes. No need for you to wait."

Rainey could hear Yusuf's deeper voice and A'aminah's voice talking softly, but she could not make out their words.

"We will go back to the front. If you are not out soon though, we will speak to Brother Khaled about you going home to rest."

Rainey waited and after a moment she turned the lock on the door and peeked out. She could see Yusuf and A'aminah walking back towards the front of the store. Rainey closed and locked the door again and called DC.

Without addressing DC, she said, "Tell me what SK wrote."

"I'll read it. Captain Jenkins faxed it to me with the ultimatum. I either locate you by 1700 hours today or the LAPD is going to put out an APB for you and have your face plastered all over national and local television news. You'll understand when I read the letter."

Rainey felt a flash of anger as her palms began to sweat inside the gloves. Her stomach rumbled and now it did feel queasy. *This can't be happening to me. SK has gone off the deep end.*

"Dear Agent Walker or shall I just address you as Rainey? I am tired of leaving messages and getting no return responses from you. Is that any way to treat an old friend? I hope you like your present. The LAPD task force is as useless and inept as the task force was in Phoenix. Only someone with a superior mind could find the Copy Cat. Me, of course. He's a sick psycho with a lust for blood. He has evaded capture after so many murders only because of the ineptitude of law enforcement. But that's why you quit the F-B-I. You are too smart, but not as smart as SK. Ha! I've had to do the task force's job for them. It took me only a week to find him.

Now it's time for you to do your duty. I will give you the name of the Copy Cat killer and tell you where he keeps his trophies, but you must come to Los Angeles. On Tuesday at noon I will phone LAPD's information hot line. The number is being shown on the television, telling the good citizens of LA to report any information on the Copy Cat killer to the task force. If you are not there when I call, the LAPD gets nothing. Copy Cat is going to be running scared after my next contact with him. He's looking for me now, but he won't find me. He doesn't know what I will do to him next. He's a coward and he's scared. He should be. If you don't answer my phone call

I'll catch up with you in your future at another place and time of my choosing. I control your future and I decide how long you live. SK"

"Jesus, DC. No wonder the task force commander is ready to explode. Jonah tried to tell him the two serial killers were linked, but no one would listen and he got tossed out on his ear. This Captain Jenkins is probably feeling the heat from the LAPD brass. And Lieutenant Jerald's caught in the cross hairs. He got the same information I gave you. Jonah thought it would satisfy his boss in Phoenix and get the lieutenant a reprieve from having to return to Phoenix."

"It sounds like you, Lieutenant Jerald and that Jonah character have been getting pretty chummy. What have you been up to, Rainey? Are you in LA? Is Jonah in LA?"

Rainey hesitated. *What should I tell DC, and how much?*

"Rainey I don't know where you are. You have got to tell me. I'll send the company jet to get you. You have got to come in. I'll go to LA with you. I believe SK will give up the Copy Cat, because she doesn't see herself as a serial killer. She believes she is on a mission and her killings are justified. In her twisted mind, she has the same opinion of the Copy Cat as you and I, and anyone else has."

Rainey sat down in a chair by the sink. As she listened to DC, she leaned against the sink feeling sick as her mind grasped the full meaning of the killer's message. *What am I going to do? I can't go to LA now. SK's coming here, could be here already. She needs to make the Six-of-Ten kill. I need some time. DC has got to buy me some time.*

"DC you have got to stall, buy me some time. I'll call you back, promise." Rainey hung up on a sputtering DC and quickly dialed Jonah.

Jonah picked up on the first ring. "I'm here with Rand. We heard your end of the conversation. We know about Jerald being taken to the LAPD headquarters. We know about the package left at the restaurant because Drew saw Jerald arrested and was about a block away when the bomb squad arrived. Later he talked to the waitress after the LAPD left. He just called me. Drew figures the package is why Jerald was hauled into the LAPD, but we were in the dark about what's happening with him and what was in the package."

Rainey described for Rand and Jonah what was in the package and filled them in on the rest. "What are we going to do?" Rainey asked.

"I don't agree with DC. I know he's the number one profiler for the FBI, but I think he's called this one wrong. SK wants you in LA so she knows where you are. She doesn't want anyone looking for her right now. She's as smart as they come. She's got DC, the Phoenix PD, and the LAPD task force focused on you and the Copy Cat. No one is looking for her. They will be waiting for her to call you at their office and they will spare no expense trying to find you. As for the Copy Cat, she's got him in a rage. I don't know what he'll do next. He may just rabbit. I figure she'll do like she wrote and contact him again to try and keep him in LA while she's in Brantlie taking care of Six-of-Ten."

"So while everyone is tracking me down and Copy Cat is hunting for SK in LA, she's here in Brantlie stalking her next victim."

"That's the way I see it, too," Rand said. "She as much as gave it away with her last sentence saying she'll find you in the future in the time and place of her choice."

"Then you don't think she intends to give up Copy Cat to the LAPD Task Force?"

"I think she intends to kill him herself and present you with her supreme accomplishment. She plans to thumb her nose at the cops the way she did in Arizona, and she wants to rub your nose in it again, Rainey," Rand concluded.

"I've been on the phone so long the battery is going out. The young woman who is breaking me in to my new job is knocking on the door for a second time and I don't think she's going to go away. I'll have to continue to pretend I'm sick so I can leave work. Do you think SK is already here?"

"It's hard to know for sure. She was in downtown LA this morning. She's set a tight schedule. She had to have done some research about Brantlie already, probably on the Internet. My first thought is she'd scope out your new uncle's place where you are staying. She'll probably show up at the store tomorrow if she doesn't make a try late this afternoon."

"We need to talk and I can't do it here and DC is waiting for a call back. Do you think I should stay here?"

"I think we need to make some decisions and we can't do it with you at the store," Jonah said.

"Rainey, I will come for you at the back of the store. Let the owner know. Leave from the back entrance in ten minutes. I'll make sure things are clear then give the okay for you to come out. If I don't give the okay, stay inside," Rand instructed Rainey.

"You can call DC as soon as Rand picks you up," Jonah said.

Rainey closed the cover of her phone, slipped it into her pocket and opened the restroom door to see a very concerned A'aminah standing in front of it with Brother Khaled. Before either could speak Rainey said, "I would like to lie down in your office and rest, Brother Khaled until Salim's wife comes for me if that is okay. I am still feeling a bit queasy."

A hard look from Rainey signaled Khaled that she needed to get to his office.

"Yes, yes, of course. That is an excellent idea." Khaled turned to A'aminah and said, "Walk with Sister Amira to my office. I have some work to do in the stock room. It will be quiet in my office and Sister Amira won't be bothered by anyone."

"Thank you Brother Khaled. I am so sorry to be so much trouble."

"No trouble at all. You take a small nap. I am sure you will feel better."

Rainey walked to the leather couch in Khaled's office and let A'aminah fuss a bit before thanking her. A'aminah turned off the lights and quietly closed the door as she left the office.

Rainey spoke to Rand. "I'm alone now. I'll leave a note for Khaled that I had to meet with you. He'll cover for me some way I am sure. If SK comes into the store, she probably won't ask for Amira and draw attention to herself. Let me finish the note to Khaled."

A few minutes later Rand said, "Rainey I'm at the back door now. All is clear. Jonah is watching from another angle."

"Coming out," Rainey said as she closed the office door behind her and walked quickly towards the back of the building. She turned left at the end of the short hallway and saw Yusuf standing at the exit door.

"I turned off the alarm temporarily and unlocked the door. I had a feeling you would need to leave by the back door when you stayed in the rest room so long," he said.

"Thank you Yusuf. I left a note for your father. Please make some excuse to A'aminah. Tell her your father sent me home and she missed seeing me leave. Would that be okay to say to her?"

"Yes that would be fine. Salaam, Rainey Walker. May Allah protect and keep you from harm."

LAPD Task Force Interrogation Room

Sunday afternoon

Lieutenant Bob Jerald sat in the interrogation room staring at a crack in the wall across from the table where he had been sitting the past two hours. The coffee in the Styrofoam cup had long gone cold.

He appeared relaxed, but his anger mounted as the minutes ticked by. He hadn't glanced once at the two-way window. He knew someone could be watching him and he wasn't going to give them the satisfaction of showing them his discomfort and humiliation at being hauled in handcuffed like a common criminal. There would be hell to pay once he talked to Major Billingsly or the Chief.

The door opened and Captain Jenkins, commander of the Task Force, walked in. Walking towards the table with a phony look of concern, he said, "Jesus Lieutenant Jerald. I'm awful sorry my boys went a little overboard. You okay? I told them to go pick you up and bring you down to the office. I had no idea they rousted you and cuffed you. I've been busy on the phones and just now heard those oafs stuck you in this room. They'll be reamed out for sure. You can count on it. I'll have them come in and apologize."

"Cut the crap, Jenkins. Those officers did exactly what they were ordered to do. I told their lieutenant and I'm telling you. I have no idea where Rainey Walker is. I have no idea where Jonah

Daniels is. I did meet with Jonah at LAX yesterday and he gave me the printouts and information I brought to the task force. Your lieutenant took the paperwork, thanked me, and told me someone from the task force would be in touch before he showed me the door. Same thing you did to Jonah Daniels. Don't do me any favors now. If I am free to go, I'll be leaving and let's not keep in touch." Lieutenant Jerald started to stand up.

"Hold on a minute, Lieutenant. You're right. I'm an asshole for laying that BS on you." Jenkins sat down in the chair opposite Lieutenant Jerald and turned his hands palms up. "Just hear me out. Give me five minutes and if you want to walk out, then I won't say another word."

Bob eased back into the chair and stared at Jenkins. Two sharp raps on the door and Jenkins yelled, "Come in." The door opened and the Sergeant in charge of the pickup detail came into the room with an armful of files, and on top of those was what looked like brown wrapping paper.

"Just put the stuff on the table and excuse yourself, Sergeant."

Bob didn't bother to watch the Sergeant leave the room. He waited for the door to close and jerked his thumb towards the two-way mirror and said, "Who you got watching us?"

"The curtain on the other side is closed and my men are all extremely busy. You'll believe me once you listen to what I have to tell you."

The Captain picked up the brown paper and slid it across the table. "What the hell!" Bob exclaimed as he read his name on the paper. "What was in the box this paper covered?"

"We think the SK killer left the box intentionally at a restaurant three blocks from headquarters." Captain Jenkins slid a stack of photographs and a sheet of paper towards Bob Jerald.

Jerald looked at a photograph of the jar with the finger immersed in it without saying anything. He picked up the photo copy of the letter addressed to Rainey and signed by SK.

"Son of a …," Jerald exclaimed. "No wonder everyone and his uncle is looking for Rainey Walker."

From that point, the captain filled Lieutenant Jerald in with all the information the task force had. When he finished, the captain looked expectantly at Lieutenant Jerald.

"Honest to God, Captain. I really don't know where Rainey is. I haven't seen her since the memorial service for her best friend, the FBI agent, who, along with Rainey's house in Arizona, was blown up by SK."

"That's what Walker's ex-boss told me and that's what your boss told me. I was just hoping they didn't know something you knew or hadn't had the opportunity to tell them, yet."

"Are you really going to put out an APB on her and have the television media plaster her face all over the evening news?"

"I don't want to, but SK is out there and I want that psycho to know we are making every effort to see that Walker is here at headquarters to answer that phone call. I think this SK killer will keep her part of the bargain. I want to get that Copy Cat killer off the streets."

"I think you need to understand something, Captain. Rainey Walker and Jonah Daniels feel even stronger about catching SK. You can't trust a psycho. They are unpredictable. What if all SK wants is to flush out Rainey so she can take a shot at her? Did any of you here think about that angle?"

"Of course we have thought of that possibility. Ms Walker will be provided police protection. There are two serial killers operating in the jurisdiction of the LAPD. We are focused on stopping both killers. We need to work together, all law enforcement agencies, and civilians like Ms. Walker and Jonah Daniels. We can't work together as long as Ms. Walker and Daniels are not part of the effort." He held up his hand. "Don't say it. I know I was part of the problem and didn't listen before. I am not going to blow off anyone else."

"The only thing I really can tell you is that I am fairly certain Rainey and Jonah with his Echo investigators are working on something that involves tracking and locating the SK serial killer. I have a business card back in the motel room with a number I can call to get in touch with Echo. That is all I have as far as any information on locating Rainey Walker or Echo."

Lieutenant Jerald watched the Captain's face redden as he moved around in the chair. Momentarily he had difficulty looking squarely at Jerald. "All your personal things at the motel were brought to headquarters. In fact your suitcase is in my office. I had them bring everything. Originally, the plan was to escort you to the airport and put you on a plane, ah, with the knowledge of your supervisor and police department."

"Let's go to your office and see if they packed that business card. You can call Jonah and give it your best shot to try and convince him and Rainey to cooperate with the LAPD. You might just consider asking them what their ideas are for locating one or both serial killers. Both are high caliber professionals, and you should think twice about working with and not against or blowing off their input. At least try this before sending out that APB and plastering Rainey's face on national television without her consent."

Captain Jenkins nodded agreement with the lieutenant, relieved that he disregarded LAPD's plan to send Jerald back to Phoenix.

The two men stood and shook hands and started for the door when a loud rap caught their attention. Before Captain Jenkins could respond, the door opened and the task force sergeant rushed in.

"All hell has broken lose, Sir. Homicide just called in that the task force needs to respond to another Copy Cat crime scene. You need to call Captain Garcia in Homicide. The lieutenant, TF team and CIS are all en route to the crime scene."

"Lieutenant Jerald, my phone call to Echo is going to have to wait."

"Want me to give it a shot? I can talk to Jonah and see if I can convince Echo and Rainey to come to LA, if they aren't in LA already."

"You can use my office. I am headed to the crime scene after I talk to Captain Garcia. I'll stop by the office if you want to ride along."

"Yes, I'd like to, and thanks, Captain. I'll be calling my boss back in Arizona and giving him an update."

"I should be ready to roll in about ten minutes." The two men left the interrogation room.

Fugitives

Sunday late afternoon

Rand, Rainey and Jonah sat inside the Command Center at an RV park on the outskirts of Brantlie. Rainey told DC that she would call him back by four to let him know if she would cooperate with the LAPD and SK. DC wasn't happy, but he knew better than to argue with her.

"Why don't I begin with a quick summary of the *players* and then each of us can state our ideas and list the scenarios we might have to deal with?"

"Sounds good to me, Jonah," Rand said.

"I have a question to pose first. Did either of you see any kind of indication that SK might be in the area now? If she came into the store I didn't spot her."

"I stuck with you, Rainey, from the time you left the bungalow until I picked you up. One of the Echo team needs to have you under constant surveillance and be in close contact all the time. Jonah arrived from LA about twenty minutes before we picked you up. Last night I identified the weak areas for potential breach by SK and left markers on Ibrahim's property. Early this morning before anyone was up and around I checked and none of the markers had been disturbed. My opinion, she was still in LA this morning and she'll probably show up sometime today and start her recon. Maybe start the stalking tomorrow."

"I agree with Rand. We're fairly certain it was SK who left the package for the LAPD Task Force in that restaurant early this morning. She had to be keeping tabs on Lieutenant Jerald also. That's what has always bothered me about SK. How does she know so much about what everyone is doing and where everybody is, except you, Rainey? You seem to have fallen off her radar and that has her worried."

"It takes the three of us at Echo to do the research, tracking, running down clues and then sometimes we miss stuff that later seems so obvious." Rand said.

'Maybe that's it. Maybe SK is in tune with the obvious and what isn't?" Rainey replied.

"Then let's start with the obvious," Jonah said as he began to type on the notebook keyboard:

- DC Britt is back at Quantico waiting for Rainey to call him.

- Echo is waiting for Drew to call in and report new intel.

- Lieutenant Jerald was taken to LAPD headquarters in handcuffs and we don't know if he is under arrest. He hasn't called the Echo number and may not be able to.

- We think SK is on her way or already here in Brantlie to stalk and kill Six-of-Ten.

- SK doesn't know where Rainey is, but wants her in LA to be sure she doesn't interfere with the stalking and killing of Six-of-Ten…we are assuming.

- The LAPD Task Force is investigating a Copy Cat serial killer who used SK as a "role model" for his killings. The TF has no evidence or information that would help identify the Copy Cat killer.

- We think SK initiated contact with the Copy Cat killer for the purpose of using him to flush out Rainey and deflect law enforcement attention away from SK. She has intentionally tried to antagonize this killer. Why?

- The San Diego PD does not believe the killing of the doctor and arson of his home is connected with SK. They believe the Black Talon ammo is nothing more than an anomaly; a quirk.

- SK has manipulated the LAPD task force to the point an APB and nationwide campaign to locate Rainey is being threatened if Rainey doesn't show up at the LAPD headquarters to accept a phone call SK said she would make revealing who Copy Cat is and where to locate him. SK's ultimatum is she won't give up the info about him unless it is to Rainey at the LAPD. Maybe?

- DC Britt is threatening to have arrest warrants taken out against Echo for obstruction unless we reveal the location of Rainey Walker.

- It is possible the LAPD will also file obstruction charges against Echo.

- SK characterized the Copy Cat killer as inept, but she discovered he has twelve kills of unknown victim ID and crime scenes. Law enforcement doesn't know much of anything about the Copy Cat killer.

- Law enforcement has identified who the SK killer is and her motivation for her killings and her victim profile is well established. She is smart, devious, a manipulator, resourceful, unpredictable, and has escaped capture in three countries.

- The LAPD and the FBI believe that SK will provide information about the Copy Cat killer if her demands are met. Why would she help law enforcement?

- Her ego; to show everyone that she is better than Copy Cat and better than law enforcement?

- SK's hatred for Copy Cat for grabbing media attention.

- SK's possible hatred for making her hunt for victims too difficult given the high profile and alert of cops and ordinary people because of the Copy Cat's murders.

- Her belief that her killings are justified and belief the Copy Cat is a cold blooded psycho killer with no justification for his killings. Maybe?

- Echo and Rainey believe SK has a different motive or plan than given by SK in letters, phone calls and pointing fingers at the Copy Cat.

- SK is using the Copy Cat to focus attention away from her so she can stalk and kill Six-of-Ten in Brantlie.

- SK wants Rainey in LA at the police department so she does not have to worry about Rainey interfering with SK's plans.

- SK made the proposal to LAPD to ensure their resources and focus were on Rainey and not SK's plans.

- SK intends to kill Copy Cat just to show everyone her superiority and because he made the mistake of trying to copy her methods of killing. She thinks he is inferior.

- If the photographs SK sent the LAPD are genuine then he is a seasoned and hardened serial killer.

- Where he has operated and who he has killed outside of the LAPD jurisdiction is unknown.

- He probably has other kills, collateral victims who didn't meet trophy kill standards but were killed for other reasons. Why? He likes to kill.

- SK set him up to be in a rage against her. She pitted herself against him and more or less challenged him to find her and kill her. Why?

- There is a high probability that SK and Copy Cat will make some considerable effort to try to kill each other.

Legal threats express or implied: Rainey

- FBI-obstruction

- LAPD –obstruction

- Consequences include: prosecution, fine and prison

- Additional charges if there are more victims and it is shown Rainey's lack of cooperation in things she said or did could have contributed.

- Loss of job, reputation, credibility as an expert in her criminal justice field.

- Potential for civil suits filed by families of victims

Legal threats express or implied: Echo

- FBI-obstruction

- LAPD obstruction

- Consequences include: prosecution, fine and prison.

- Additional charges if there are more victims and lack of cooperation in things echo could have contributed.
- Additional charges related to Echo operations and investigative work.
- Loss of PI licenses.
- Loss of weapons permits.
- Loss of business-bankruptcy.
- Potential for civil suits filed by families of victims

The crux of our immediate problem is:

A. We shut down the operation in Brantlie, losing any opportunity to capture SK and save at minimum, five lives plus any lives SK could take as collateral damage. We take Rainey to the LAPD and do our best to keep her safe from SK and perhaps the Copy Cat.

B. We stay in Brantlie and continue the operation, anticipating that SK will take the bait. This means accepting the consequences from law enforcement. This scenario could result in not indentifying and capturing the Copy Cat killer.

Jonah, Rand and Rainey seemed to run out of steam at this point. "Anything else we can add to this team assessment?" Jonah asked. Rainey and Rand nodded no.

"Drew should have called in already. It's unlike him not to. Should we give him a call?" Rand asked Jonah.

"Yes. Before we decide and Rainey calls DC, I'd like his input. I'll call him," Jonah said as he flipped open his cell phone.

Rand's attention went back to the monitors. He had been researching serial killings in the USA and abroad, looking for a pattern that might link to the Copy Cat. Rainey noticed that some of the databases Rand was accessing could be problematic, but she didn't say anything. Rand switched to local, national, and world news channels.

"Drew what's up? We've been waiting on your call? What? Hold on." Jonah turned to Rand and said, "Get the local LA station, CNN, and Fox up on the screens."

"Go ahead, Drew"

"About 2:30 this afternoon I am casually hanging out at a cigar stand where I can see the parking exit of the LAPD, waiting to see if Lieutenant Jerald gets released. I see about a half dozen cop cars with lights and sirens come screaming out and they all head north. So I jump in my car parked a couple hundred feet away and discretely follow. The radio traffic is jammed and then it settles down to normal traffic. The Code 3 officers have switched to a closed frequency. The cops all stop in front of the Waldorf Hotel and before I know it, the street is shut down to police-only traffic. I circle the block and find a place to park, then hoof it back to a coffee shop next door to the Waldorf. I hang out looking for the right person to ask what's going on. About twenty minutes later, the LAPD Copy Cat TF shows up. So I go out and start milling around at the edges of the crowd that has gathered. I hear some lady say a woman has been killed in one of the apartments, not the short term guest hotel rooms, but long term tenants that rent on the upper floors. I look at the huge glass doors of the Waldorf and can see through into the lobby area. A couple of detectives are grilling the doorman. I figured I'd wait around and make contact with the doorman and get what details I can pick up."

"Where are you at now Drew?"

"I'm sitting in the coffee shop, and Lieutenant Jerald is sitting across from me having a cup of java."

"What? How'd he get to a crime scene and hell, Drew, he doesn't even know you." Jonah spoke a lot louder than he'd intended. Rand and Rainey were staring at Jonah.

"Like I said, I was standing at the edges of the crowd, and an unmarked LAPD vehicle drives up and parks in the middle of the street in front of the Waldorf. Big as life, Lieutenant Jerald opens the passenger door and gets out of this unmarked. The driver who gets out just happens to be the task force commander, Captain Jenkins. Can you believe that shit? They haul in this Phoenix cop, then hours later he shows up at the next crime scene."

"So how did you end up having coffee with him?" Jonah's tone betrayed his impatience.

"I'm getting to that," Drew replied. "I see the lieutenant looking around at the crowd like all cops do, and I holler out "Echo" and then "Rainey W." I stand a good five inches over most people, so he sees me and makes a bee line for where I'm standing. He asks if my name is Drew. I say yes, and I show him the Echo hard card. I tell him I'll be waiting in the coffee shop for him when he gets done at the crime scene. So here we are sitting in the coffee shop, and he's patiently waiting to talk to you."

"Hold on a minute, Drew." Jonah notices that Rand and Rainey are watching the Copy Cat stories on breaking news. "Did you pickup that Drew is having coffee with Bob Jerald and that he wants to talk?" Rand and Rainey nodded.

"Hand Bob the phone, Drew. I'll talk with him."

Agreement

Sunday early evening

The phone call to DC did not go well.
Rainey knew it wouldn't because she refused to tell him where she was. He was only partially mollified when she told him she had agreed to be at the LAPD headquarters before noon on Tuesday.

The conversation between Jonah and Bob had gone much better, and Captain Jenkins had the grace to thank Rainey, through Lieutenant Jerald, for cooperating with the Copy Cat investigation at some personal risk to herself.

"I still think that Jerald and the LAPD are holding something back. I don't know if it has to do with SK, the Copy Cat or both." Jonah said.

"Ya know, I got that same feeling. Maybe it's just that we aren't cops. Out of the business, in their opinion. They think of us as civilians and they don't want to share anything they think that civilians don't need to know," Rand mused.

Rainey's voice carried some bitterness when she commented, "Cops even treat other cops that way, too, Rand. They have some kind of thing. It isn't even a macho thing, because female cops do it, too. They like to horde information, and sometimes they are blind as to how that affects an investigation."

Jonah winced, but sucked it up. "Sometimes cops just want to win so bad, and sometimes a case becomes political to the brass."

"And I thought the military was bad," Rand exclaimed.

"Let's get back to business, shall we?" Jonah said, changing the uncomfortable subject. Rand and Rainey took their cue from Jonah.

"I really think if SK is going to come after a Six-of-Ten here in Brantlie, it will be tomorrow."

"How can you be so sure, Rainey? Maybe you just want her to make the try tomorrow because you agreed to show up at LAPD headquarters before noon on Tuesday. Maybe SK didn't see the article in the *Brantlie Muslim Voice* and we're just spinning our wheels?"

"Hold on Rand. We have a good plan and we did all the assessments we always do and the probability that SK would take the bait was pretty damn high, else we wouldn't have invested so much or gotten the Muslim community's hopes up, either. They have a lot invested in this besides money and resources. They've made a lot of sacrifices already."

"No, Jonah, Rand's right to question. I originally thought it would be Tuesday, but Monday is a better choice. SK plans to call me in LA on Tuesday and gloat about making her Six-of-Ten kill when she calls. She probably thinks I'll be traveling from the East Coast to LA on Monday."

"We'll stay hunkered down here in Brantlie if she doesn't make a try on Amira before Rainey leaves on Tuesday. If SK doesn't call the LAPD on Tuesday, Rainey is under no obligation to remain in LA, and she isn't under any obligation to tell anyone where she is going." Jonah stated.

"As far as I am concerned the LAPD and the FBI will be told I'm taking a vacation to a destination unknown. I'm coming back here to finish it with SK if nothing happens tomorrow."

"Then we are staying and seeing this through," Rand replied and Jonah agreed.

"When I go to LA Tuesday, you will stay and do surveillance on the Sultana store. Jonah will do surveillance on Ibrahim's place. Jonah can have Drew drive to Brantlie so he can accompany me to LA. Captain Jenkins already knows him. I just hope Drew kept our location off the radar. I don't think he could have been persuaded to share it with Lieutenant Jerald or that task force commander."

"We can count on Drew. He's solid. The jury is still out on Bob Jerald. He is still a working cop and he's got that retirement to be worried about. The lines for him are pretty much drawn, and he does have to follow orders," Jonah remarked.

"Are you supposed to work tomorrow, Rainey?"

"The store will be open from nine in the morning until seven. I plan on staying all day. In the note I left for Mr. Khaled, I said that I would be back at work tomorrow. I'll have to call Ibrahim and let him know what we think will happen tomorrow."

"Just don't go to the back of the store by yourself. Stay up front where there are people. I doubt if she'd try anything with so many people around. The Muslim men were well intentioned, but they've done such a good job of securing Ibrahim's property, SK might not chance a strike there. Too many people watching there and at the store," Jonah said, as he continued to study a map spread out on the table.

"So where do you think she'll try to take out Amira?"

Jonah put his index finger on the map where Ibrahim's house location was circled. He then traced the route that Ibrahim used to drive Rainey to the Sultana Store. "Salim's wife is driving Rainey back and forth from home to work each day. Two women alone and without a male accompanying them. When she struck in the past she always made sure the men were nowhere around."

Rand looked at the route Jonah had traced and began writing at different places along the route. He pulled up MapQuest and typed in the two addresses. "That's a little over seven miles. Too many miles for just the two of us to watch. Even with Drew, there's just too much space, too many places she could be laying in wait."

"You think she'll try to get us stopped in some way and then what? Take us at gun point? To where?" Rainey was now studying the map. "I never thought about that. About Salim's wife driving Amira. She's in danger driving me."

"I agree. If the plan is forcing Salim's wife off the road and taking Amira at gunpoint to some unknown location, then I'm pretty sure she'd kill Salim's wife right away and leave her with the car."

Rainey blanched when she heard this straightforward description of how SK might kill Saba.

Rand looked over at Jonah and found Jonah staring at him. Jonah didn't blink. Rainey noticed Jonah staring, too.

"What are you thinking, Jonah?" Rand asked.

"I'm thinking Rainey needs to call Ibrahim and ask for a head scarf, gloves, veil, and abeya to fit a person five-foot-seven. Your tennis shoes will do just fine, Rand."

The look of consternation on Rand's face was priceless. Rainey burst into a fit of laughter. Rand got a mulish look on his face and said, "I am not dressing up, Jonah."

Jonah tried hard to keep his face serious but grinned, "Oh, yes you are, Rand. You are going to be Rainey's pretend Muslim driver."

Rainey was grinning as she looked at her wrist watch. It was almost four o'clock. "I better call DC and let him know I'll be there on Tuesday. If we get SK tomorrow, we won't have to worry about the LAPD. Then I'll call Ibrahim so he can get the clothes ready and wait at the mosque for Rand." Rainey saw the frown on Rand's face, but he nodded agreement.

"While you two are busy I'm going to cook us some supper. I'll give Drew a call after we eat."

"Sounds good to me. I never did learn how to cook despite my grandmother's best efforts."

Jonah handed Rainey a new cell phone and she dialed DC's number.

* * *

"What's keeping Rand?" Jonah grumbled. Dinner had been ready for well over an hour. Rainey had called Ibrahim and brought him up to date. Ibrahim said he would take the clothes to the mosque for Rand. He said he planned on going there to speak with security and Salim about his wife staying indoors for the next few days.

"Why not call Rand?" Rainey asked as she eyed the food on the table hungrily.

"And get told he's a big boy now and doesn't need a mother anymore?"

"Maybe he got to talking with the brothers at the mosque, or he had to wait for Ibrahim?" Rainey offered in a neutral tone.

"It's about time," Jonah said to Rand as he entered the Command Center carrying a large bag boasting the words *Sultana Books & More.*

"It's not my fault. Rainey. These Muslims are so courteous I am amazed. I was waiting at the mosque for Ibrahim to arrive. He was late because he stopped at the store to buy me new clothing. He told me it was the very least he should do for me as I was forced to dress as a woman. He did not want me to have to wear used clothing."

"So you got a brand new outfit, did ya? Are you going to model for us?" Jonah said trying to keep a straight face.

Rainey wasn't able to hold her laughter. Rand looked even grumpier than when he left, and Jonah's teasing wasn't helping.

"Leave it alone, Jonah or you'll see an increase in my share of Echo profits."

Jonah burst out laughing. "Profits?"

Rand looked at Rainey and then back at Jonah. Jonah was doubled over laughing. Slowly the frown lines disappeared and Rand started laughing, too.

Rainey wiped the tears from her eyes and offered to warm up the food. Rand and Jonah looked at her as if she had lost it.

"I'm so hungry I'm not waiting," Rand said as he sat at the table and started to fill his plate. Jonah sat down, mimicking Rand.

Rainey sat down and started to fill her plate. "A good thing because I'd probably burn it."

The Package

Sunday evening

A'aminah sighed. She looked at the clock on the wall. Only twenty minutes until closing. She was tired as it had been a very long day for her. Brother Khaled had to leave the store early for an important meeting and had asked her if she could stay with Sister Maryam and Brother Yusuf to close the store. Of course she had agreed. She wasn't married. She didn't have a husband or children to go home to look after as the other sisters did.

A'aminah saw the headlamps of a large vehicle shine through the glass in the front doors. She walked towards the front to greet whoever had stopped to make a purchase so late. It must be something important as most of the time the store was empty the last thirty minutes before closing. This gave the employees time to do some housekeeping for the next day.

When the driver turned off the headlamps, A'aminah saw that the vehicle was a dark colored SUV. She watched as the driver's door opened. A special lift with a sister in a wheelchair was lowered until the wheels touched the pavement. The sister then shut the driver's side door to the SUV. A'aminah hurried to open the door as Brother Khaled had not yet installed the type of doors needed for the disabled. The sister in the wheelchair was covered in black abeya, hijab, gloves and veil. Her back was bent forward in the chair. A'aminah thought she must be an elderly sister.

"As Salaam'Alaykum Sister. Thank you for your help," the old woman greeted A'aminah in a voice that had a slight quaver to it.

"Wa alaykum as salaam," A'aminah replied.

"I know it is late. Being an old woman, I took a nap and over-slept. I arrived at the masjid late for prayer and then I did not get the opportunity to greet the new sister to our community, Brother Ibrahim's niece. I have a gift for her."

"Sister Amira was at work earlier today but became ill and went home. I don't think you missed her, Sister. I don't think she went to the masjid this evening. I am not sure if she will be at work tomorrow," Sister A'aminah told the old woman. *What a dear she is to make such a kind effort.*

"I am leaving in the morning for a trip to my homeland and will be gone all summer. I thought I would just drive here and leave the gift for her. The newspaper article said she would be working here this summer. I do not know where Brother Ibrahim lives and did not want to be driving around at night looking for his home and disturb the family. I don't care to drive to far at night. I recently moved here myself, and live just a few miles from the store."

"You must have moved into the Bright Days Community. Many older people and also the disabled reside there. I have heard that the management and staff offer excellent services. My good friend told me that the small houses and apartments are especial-ly designed for the handicapped. She works there doing gardening work."

"Ah... let me see... could your friend be... ah... I am thinking..."

"Would it be sister Aneerah you are thinking of?" A'aminah suggested.

"Yes. Thank you, Sister?"

"Oh, I am sorry. I did not introduce myself. I am Sister A'aminah."

"Pleased to meet you. I am Sister Amatullah." The two women nodded to each other.

"The assisted living community is very nice. I immigrated here over twenty years ago. I was injured in an automobile accident shortly after I arrived. I have no family here in this country. I have been independent these many years and I appreciate having a place like the Bright Days Community."

How difficult it must be not to have an extended Muslim family. *No wonder this dear lady wanted to meet Sister Amira and give her a welcoming gift,* A'aminah thought. She looked at the brown paper wrapped package on top of the old woman's lap. "Would you like to leave the gift with me? I can put it in the office and if Sister Amira comes to work tomorrow I will be sure to give it to her."

"It is not much, only a book I thought she might enjoy."

"Sister Amira loves books. She has been assigned to work in the book section. A book is really the perfect gift for her. I know she will be so pleased to receive your gift."

"This is so kind of you, Sister A'aminah," the old woman said as she handed the wrapped package to A'aminah. "Oh my, it is now just a few minutes until you close and I have kept you here talking. I must go and let you finish up. May Allah reward you for your kindness and for spending some time talking with this old woman."

The old woman patted A'aminah's arm and then turned the electric-powered wheelchair while A'aminah held the door for her. A'aminah watched as the driver's door opened and the lift came out and lowered to pavement level.

A'aminah watched until the SUV was traveling out of the parking lot. She walked back inside, closed and locked the door, placing the closed sign on the door.

Maryam and Yusuf, finishing their work in different parts of the store, walked to the front of the store and watched A'aminah lock the door. Yusuf noticed that the trash bags were still sitting in the aisles. Yusuf asked, "Sister A'aminah, why were you standing outside when we needed to finish the work and close up? The trash bags are still in the aisles. Sister Maryam has finished with the accounts and I have secured the store except the door you just locked."

Sister A'aminah's cheeks turned red and she lowered her eyes in embarrassment at Brother Yusuf's mild rebuke and said nothing about the old woman. "I am sorry. I will hurry and finish up. There are only the trash bags to take to the back. I will do this right away."

Brother Yusuf cringed. *I have embarrassed Sister A'aminah.* He felt awful about doing it. He admired the sister for her hard work and many kindnesses he had seen her do at the store and on the campus at school. She was greatly admired for her good manners and her knowledge of the Qur'an and hadith. Yusuf had been considering talking to his parents about broaching a formal marriage proposal to her. He had hesitated as he was unsure if she would consider him. He still had two years of university to complete. He was not sure how A'aminah would feel about marrying him or if her parents who lived in Chicago would approve of him. Maybe Sis A'aminah did not want to marry right now? Maybe she decided she would wait until she finishes university? These questions he had been thinking and praying about for some months. *Now I have embarrassed her and been unkind. I am an oaf.*

Yusuf quickly recovered and said softly, "My apologies Sister A'aminah. It is not a problem. I will take care of the bags. You can wait here with Sister Maryam. Her husband will be here in a few minutes to take both of you home."

Family Dinner
Sunday evening

"This is Mr. James Thornton. Yes, the penthouse. I have an important meeting in the morning and I cannot be late. I'd appreciate it if you would have my car ready out front at eight AM. Also, I've had to cancel a dinner at my grandfather's as I am still a bit under the weather." James faked a cough and roughened his voice even more. "Could you please hold all calls this evening? I'm having an early night. Yes and thank you. You have a pleasant evening, too."

James left the penthouse as planned and arrived at Christopher's apartment without running into anyone at either apartment building. He walked to the master bedroom and placed his newest trophy on the bedroom dresser. He changed his clothing and with wig, contact lenses, and makeup transformed himself into Christopher. Taking a last look in the mirror and saluting Christopher, he walked back to the living room and picked up the phone.

James dialed his Grandfather's home. "Grandfather." He waited, listening patiently until his grandfather paused.

"No, nothing like that. I've been delayed with an important business matter. I won't arrive until about eight thirty. Is that too late?" James waited until the old man fawned some more and then interrupted him.

"Good. You and Dad go ahead and start without me. I'll try to make it in time for dessert. Yes, I know my father will be upset. He's always upset about something I did or didn't do. Thank you, Grandfather. I'll see you as soon as I can."

"Grandfather will be so pleased, Christopher. You will arrive only a few minutes late. Oh, I am sorry. I forgot. Grandfather didn't invite you. Of course he and father won't be real happy to meet you, will they?"

The drive to his grandfather's home was forty-five minutes from Christopher's apartment. Grandfather had been paying for James' penthouse and unknowingly paid for Christopher's apartment, too. *One of the perks of being a company VP*, James thought.

James planned on using his house key to let himself in. If the butler saw him, then Christopher would be the last thing he saw. His plan was really very simple. He'd walk back to the dining room where his grandfather and father would be eating their first course. The room would be filled with their silence as both men would be concentrating on their food to avoid having to make small talk. His grandfather would be watching the clock and waiting anxiously for his dear boy James to arrive.

What a big surprise for Grandfather and dear old Dad. Instead of James walking into the dining room it would be Christopher pointing the gun and shooting both of them dead. James smirked as he played out the scenario in his head, checking his murder kit to make sure he had packed the silencer and extra clip.

A home invasion and robbery is what the cops would tell him resulted in the deaths of his family. The safe would have been opened and cleaned out. They would tell him his father put up a tremendous struggle. A painting would be slashed and near priceless crystal smashed. The remains of the dinner would be scattered on the floor amid the blood and glass. The butler, who had been with his grandfather for years, would be found shot in the head in the kitchen. Tragic.

James almost wet himself playing out the events that would happen in less than an hour. His blood lust was high, and he could not wait to appease it. His revenge against his father would be complete.

The family dinner had gone just as planned. James parked the Bentley in the airport lot, locked it, and retrieved the suitcase from the trunk. His grandfather's travel suitcase had been a handy find, useful for packing the cash and jewelry he stole from the old man's safe.

He wheeled the suitcase through the parking lot to the closest passenger pickup area, where he flagged down a taxi. Relaxing in the back seat, he gave the driver directions to the storage place so he could get the pickup and handcart. He still had to pack the trunks and stage the apartment for when the cops finally got around to entering Christopher's apartment, hoping to find the Copy Cat. James covered his mouth to silence his giggles.

The taxi pulled in front of the storage place. James paid the cab fare, got out, and lifted the suitcase out of the back seat. He waited until the driver pulled away before using the keypad that deactivated the gate lock.

Driving the pickup truck he kept in storage, James arrived at Christopher's apartment building. He parked in the rear in a guest parking slot to avoid the night security. With the suitcase strapped to the handcart, he made his way uninterrupted to the back entrance and elevators. He pushed the up arrow for the waiting elevator that would take him to the tenth floor.

James opened Christopher's apartment door, flipped on the light, and shut and locked the door behind him. He pulled the cart and suitcase behind him into the master bedroom, where his newest trophy waited. That one wouldn't be going with the others, he had decided. He'd leave it with the silencer for the cops to find. Proof that Christopher was the Copy Cat killer. James laughed as he said, "The elusive Copy Cat killer."

James took fresh clothing from the closet and laid it on the bed. He went into the bathroom for a fast shower. Feeling refreshed as he towel-dried his hair, his excitement began to rise. He dressed quickly. Every time he visited his beauties he felt this familiar tingling and warm sensation. James picked up the key ring from the bed and walked over to the walk-in closet door. He unlocked the door, opened it, and flipped on the light. His eyes feasted on the shelves. He walked forward and the soft lighting came on caressing the beauties he had worked so joyously to procure."No! No!" The words tore from his throat as he screamed and rushed closer to the trophy case.

Rage tore through him. His eyes were blinded by flashes of white heat. And from deep inside, James felt fear. It grabbed him and shook his body. He began to tremble violently as his gaze swept the room. There was no one in it save himself. But she had been here. "SK!" He howled her name out loud as feelings of impotency threatened to smother him. James pressed the jar he held to his chest and slowly recounted the crystal jars. Fourteen. The one missing was Copy Cat Trophy Number Three.

Think. Think! Was anything else disturbed in the apartment? James looked at the shelves where he stored his weapons, ammo, and poisons. "Nothing else is missing. Only the third Copy Cat trophy." James unconsciously began grinding his teeth in agitation. He looked at the three steamer trunks with the closed lids. He bent forward and reached his hand toward the first trunk and quickly pulled his hand back as if he had been burned. *What if she planted a bomb?* James shook his head from side to side as if trying to shake his fear. He sucked in his breath and slowly opened each trunk. They were empty like he had left them.

Slowly James sank to his knees and leaned back against the wall as he tried to concentrate. *I'm not safe here. I don't know who she is, yet she found me. I must leave. I should never have come back to this country.* James gathered his strength and slowly stood. He hated her with a passion and wanted her dead, but his fear of her was even greater. *I'll pack the trunks, stage the apartment and leave. I'll store the trunks for now at the storage shed. I can get them shipped overseas later. I'll telephone the airlines and get the first available flight to Europe. I'll have to get my papers from the penthouse. I'll transfer grandfather's money using the passbooks. I'll be long gone before it's missed. The cops will be looking for me, but won't have figured anything out in time. They'll be too busy tracking down the Copy Cat. I'll wait at the airport until my flight is called.*

He kept telling himself that he hoped she had the guts to show her face, but deep inside he knew all his frantic planning was really because he was running from SK. *Where is she? Is she coming back here?*

James realized he was unarmed. He rushed out of the closet and dashed towards his bed and the murder kit. Fear paralyzed him momentarily. He grabbed his weapon from the kit and returned to the closet, packing the trunks while keeping an eye on the bedroom door. James worked frantically, but every sound, real or imagined, caused his shattered nerves to set off a fresh round of fear. When he finished packing two of the trunks, he dragged them to the living room, leaving them close to the front door. James left all the trophies and some of the weapons and ammo. Now he shuddered each time he looked at those trophies. They reminded him of how stupid he had been about SK. He went into the bathroom and feverishly began removing any trace of James Thornton. He needed to take his trunks and get out of the apartment. He'd do the bedroom last. James was in such a frenzy, mumbling to himself, and with shaking hands he hurried to finish wiping down the room. He failed to hear the front door to the apartment open and quietly shut.

SK – Unfinished Business
Monday early morning

The ride had been exhilarating. The machine handled beautifully. At midnight, traffic was light and the cops almost non-existent. She had pushed the speed on some stretches of the highway to one hundred miles per hour and cut thirty minutes from her travel time. Midnight, and she was almost there.

The parking security officer at the apartment complex was startled from his light snooze by the revving of the motorcycle as it pulled up to the gate. Not much happened after midnight, especially transitioning from Sunday night to early Monday morning.

The parking security officer's eyes took in the gleaming hog stopped at the gate. The motorcycle was an attention getter for sure. What was capturing his attention, though, was not the gleaming purple and silver machine with the bright orange flames. No. His attention was fixed on the rider sitting on the machine. The rider was wearing a helmet with a dark tinted visor, a form-fitting one piece jump suit and riding boots. Helmet and jump suit were purple and silver with an orange flame pattern. The rider and machine looked like they were a part of each other.

The rider reached up, lifted off the helmet and shook out her long silver hair. "George, my man. How ya doing?"

The security officer's face split into a look of amazement and then a big grin. "Ms. Stewart, is that really you? Sure it is. What a surprise."

"Like this hog and my fancy duds, do you? I just got this beauty two days ago. I've been riding all over California. I had it on order with the riding clothes for almost three months. I take it you like?"

"The Honda is a beaut and you look smashing, Ms. Stewart. I didn't know you were into riding. Just caught me by surprise."

"I've got a very early morning appointment, George, so if you can let me through…."

"Oh, sorry, Ms. Stewart" George depressed the lock and the gate slid open.

SK rode into the parking garage and parked her bike in the space she usually parked her SUV.

She got off the elevator on the 8th floor and walked down the plush carpeted hallway to Room 802. Unlocking the door, she flipped on the overhead light and set down the small suitcase. She began carefully walking through the interior of each room making sure the rooms were empty and had not had any unwanted visitors. Now was not the time for her to break habits. It had paid off in the past to be careful.

She checked to make sure there weren't any planted cameras or listening devices, though she didn't think Jimmy-boy could have pulled himself together enough to locate her in Christopher's building and then set a trap.

SK was tired. She had little sleep in the last four days and had put hundreds of miles on the SUV and her bike. She could not rest. Not now when there was still much to do and only a few hours to take care of the unfinished business.

Her head began to ache and the voice decided to make an appearance. *What about Rainey? What about Six-of-Ten? All you think about is that damn Copy Cat!*

"I can take care of Rainey Walker anytime I choose. I enjoy making her dance to my tune. Don't harp on and on about her. When I get tired of making her and her friends jump hoops I'll end it my way and at my time."

The voice came back more stridently, *She made a fool of you. Five months of healing after surgery and another six months, and still no Six-of-Ten and the rest are left walking and breathing and the men who died are not avenged.*

Ignoring the voice and the sharp pain and accompanying white noise, SK reached for the suitcase, opened it, and gently took out the small delicately embroidered pillow. She unzipped the end and withdrew the trophy for Five-of-Ten and stroked it while reliving the moments of triumph when she took it from the heathen.

Again the voice intruded on her pleasure, *Your mission is failing. You have been outsmarted and have done nothing. Nothing!* the voice shrieked demanding SK's attention.

"It's that Copy Cat-Jimmy-boy. He got the cops all riled up. He is the one drawing attention to Muslims and got the Muslim communities to go on alert. He's the one who destroyed all the plans I made before I even left Arizona. He's mocked my work with his phony Post-it notes and killing women for his blood lust. He has to pay for this. Now leave me alone. I must finish it tonight," SK shouted back at the voice.

She placed the trophy back inside the pillow and closed the zipper. Ignoring the pain and increasing white noise filling her mind, SK returned the pillow to the suitcase and took off the jumpsuit and boots.

SK went to the video setup in the living room. "Let's see how Jimmy-boy reacted to the loss of one of his precious trophies."

Not So Nice to Meet You
Monday early morning

SK dressed in a black long-sleeved pullover shirt and black jeans. She padded over to the dresser, took out a black pair of socks, and sat down on the corner of the bed to put them on and a pair of black rubber soled shoes. She placed a pair of camel-skinned gloves on the bed with a black veil that had an opening for only the eyes. SK learned that latex gloves left fingerprints on the inside and stopped using them several years ago. The gloves were thin and fit like a second skin.

From the small suitcase she withdrew a black utility belt and placed it across the bed. She took out a .22 and silencer from a black travel kit within, and loaded it with Black Talon ammo found in a pocket of the suitcase. She took a 6-inch serrated knife and its sheaf, a heat-seeking device, and a dart gun loaded with a tranq drug and laid it next to the .22. She reached inside another side pocket and took out a loaded hypodermic needle and placed it in a specially made holder on the utility belt. The last item was the stolen apartment key card to Carrington's apartment which she slipped into a front pocket of her jeans. Satisfied, she closed the small suitcase, placing it inside the open and empty larger suitcase laid out on the bed.

SK placed the weapons in the specially designed holsters on the utility belt and then fastened the belt around her waist. She picked up the heat-seeking device and slung the strap over her shoulder. She had bought the ingenious device on the black market. The asshole who sold it to her said it came from Russia, but it was made in Israel. He grossly overcharged, but she paid the man. She caught up with him at another time and place and retrieved what she had paid and then some. He wasn't around anymore to cheat anyone else.

SK looked around the apartment, deciding to finish her packing. She placed the long silver hair wig, notebook computer, and the video tape of Copy Cat going nuts inside his trophy room into the larger suitcase. Her travel clothes were laid out next to the suitcase waiting for when she got ready to leave the hotel.

Everything else would be left in the room for the cops to gather as evidence and waste their time examining. They would be interested in the camera and video equipment. She wanted them to know she had been in this room staying in the same building as Christopher Carrington-Copy Cat. *Too bad Jimmy-boy won't know I've been living here right under his nose. Maybe I'll tell him?* SK laughed out loud.

SK put on the gloves and the face veil. She was ready for her visit. She opened the front door to the apartment. The hallway was clear. She walked quickly to the Exit door and stairwell and began climbing the two flights of stairs to the tenth floor.

SK had cleaned up after her messy visit and put on the clothes she'd laid out on the bed. It was a little after four AM. She telephoned for a taxi, then left the apartment taking the elevator down to the lobby pulling the extra large travel suitcase on wheels behind her. She was smiling and thinking, *Thank you Jimmy-boy for the suitcase and all the lovely cash.* She walked through the lobby doors as the taxi pulled up to the curb. She gave him the directions to an all night restaurant located a block from the storage facility location. *Time to pick up the SUV and store my luggage in it.*

* * *

SK walked through the rooms of Jimmy-boy's penthouse apartment. There was nothing much of interest except the notebook she found on the dining room table and an airline ticket, passport for a Mr. Thom Kruger, and a wallet with a couple of Visa cards with Thom Kruger's name and about $1,500 in cash. SK took out the cash and jammed it in her jeans pocket.

The flight date for the airplane reservation puzzled SK momentarily. "Now why would Jimmy-boy schedule a flight for two weeks from yesterday?" A sly grin turned up the corners of her lips as she nodded her head. "Of course. He intended to spend those two weeks looking for and killing me before he left for Germany!"

She sat down at the dining room table and turned the computer on. Clicking on the Internet icon SK quickly looked through his favorites list out of curiosity. "Ah, Jimmy-boy you planned your escape and it would have been important that your trophies escape with you."

It was easy now to joke about the Copy Cat. The voice, white noise, and pain had remained silent since she left the apartment she had leased under the name of Elaine Stewart.

SK clicked on the site she was looking for and found the address. SK committed it to memory and shut down the Internet. She'd take Jimmy-boy's notebook with her. She stood and took one more look around the room and then walked out the front door, not bothering to close or lock it.

SK rode the dumbwaiter down to the kitchen. Carefully opening the door and seeing no one around, walked out of it. She went through the swinging door to the store room and from there she walked to the exit door, opened it, and went outside and stood briefly in the alleyway while she pulled off the gloves and jammed them into a pocket. It was almost daybreak. She walked to her SUV parked a few feet from the door, unlocked it, and climbed inside. She drove the SUV to the end of the alleyway and turned right. SK's thoughts were already moving ahead to the hunt for Six of Ten.

Operation SK - Day 2
Monday morning - Brantlie

Rainey finished the last set of leg lifts and got to her feet just in time to answer the ringing of her cell phone.

"Good morning, Rainey. Wanted to let you know that there weren't any indications of SK doing surveillance around the property last night or early this morning."

"Morning, Jonah. I don't know if that is good or not. It seems strange that nothing's happened here since that article was run in the paper. Maybe SK missed it?"

"Not likely she missed it. We know she's here in California and was in LA when she left that package. She could still be in LA or here in Brantlie. I talked with Ibrahim last night and he told me the *Brantlie Muslim Voice* is distributed to all the mosques. If she's watching the mosques then she would have access to the paper."

"Did Drew get in last night? I was so tired last evening. I was sorry I had to leave before he arrived, but I'm a working girl." Rainey tried to lighten the mood as much for Jonah as herself.

"That is the other reason I called. Drew stayed in LA. I agreed with his assessment of the situation. With Rand driving you and since we have the help of the Muslim security I told him we could hold the fort here. SK stalked her victims in Arizona for a week or more before she decided to act. It's been just a couple of days since the article was published."

"Maybe she'll make her move tomorrow when she expects me to be in Los Angles. She may be watching this bungalow or the store waiting for an opportunity. Maybe we've made it too secure?"

"We don't know what precautions we've taken she could be aware of. The fence at Ibrahim's place is logical and I don't think it would arouse any suspicions with SK. There's no additional security at the store that she could know about. I think it's just a waiting game for us and we need to stay alert." Jonah waited as Rainey didn't answer right away.

"This constant wondering. Will she strike today? Will it be tomorrow? She loves these games she plays and manipulates us all," Rainey said. She took a deep breath. "I think we got side tracked. You were going to tell me why Drew stayed in LA."

"Right. Late yesterday Bob Jerald called him and they agreed to meet at Jerald's motel room. He wanted to talk about the latest Copy Cat killing. Drew said he's sure he didn't tell him everything, but enough to raise some red flags with Drew."

"He's still on the payroll so we can't expect him to give out a lot of details about an ongoing investigation, Jonah."

"I know. That's why Drew was surprised at the invitation."

"Maybe they don't trust my word about showing up tomorrow and LAPD wants to pump Drew to find out where I am."

"That's what I thought until Drew told me what they talked about. This last killing by the Copy Cat deviated from the others. He shot the woman and placed a Post-it note on her forehead. He covered the face with a Muslim-type scarf and he cut off a pinkie finger and took it with him. Drew said there wasn't any forced entry either so that was the same. What was different was the condition of the victim's body. Drew said the bedroom was wrecked. It looked like the Copy Cat was in one hell of a rage and took it out on the victim. He beat the hell out of the woman post mortem. He kicked her in the rib cage, cracking four ribs and he smashed her face with a blunt object, breaking her nose and fracturing her cheek bones. What was really unusual was that he left the victim on the floor naked instead of posing her fully dressed on the bed as he did the other three victims."

"Do you think SK's manipulations of the Copy Cat could be behind the rage Drew described?"

"Jerald said as much to Drew and implied that Captain Jenkins is leaning towards that assumption. Drew said that Captain Jenkins thinks they may have a lead. The first one since the killings started. When they did the interviews with the doorman and valet on duty last night, both mentioned a rich guy driving a silver Bentley coming to the hotel and leaving within the time frame the coroner has established for death."

"What made this guy stand out more than other guests arriving and leaving?" Rainey asked.

"He over-tipped and the Bentley was a honey of a car. Not that many vintage Bentleys around, and the valet was excited about driving it. Drew said Jerald said the detective doing the interview had a hell of a time getting the kid to focus on the driver description. All he seemed to remember was the two $10 tips and getting to drive and park the Bentley."

"If they think this rich guy is a possible for the Copy Cat, I don't know. Seems like a long shot. I mean why would he make himself so visible by driving a Bentley and over-tipping? It doesn't make sense." Rainey commented.

"Nothing about the Copy Cat has made sense. And having some kind of relationship with SK? It is just off the wall. I've never run across anything like this here or in Europe or any place else I've done investigations involving serial killers."

"We started out about a week ago with a straight forward plan. Establish me as bait and set a trap for SK. We've made no headway with SK and this Copy Cat keeps cropping up," Rainey said.

"Drew said the detectives are trying to track down the Bentley from a partial plate number the doorman remembered. They checked out one that seemed a possible. The registration was to a guy named Harold Carrington but this guy came up deceased. They don't know what happened to this guy's Bentley. He didn't elaborate much more on this. Things are really busy. You know how it is in the first twenty four hours after a homicide happens."

"Yeah, I do. I was thinking, though, that car might have been sold and not reregistered or a family member inherited the car," Rainey offered.

"Drew said he mentioned that, but you know in this kind of investigation every lead, slim or not, has to be checked out."

"So we stick to our plan for Tuesday?"

"With Drew staying in LA, I'll travel with you to LA tomorrow and Rand will stay here to keep an eye on things. You'll go to work as usual and leave in a delivery truck disguised as one of the delivery men. Drew will come back with us after you get through at the LAPD. Whether SK phones or doesn't, at one o'clock you'll leave with Drew and meet up with me at an arranged location. Drew will know where. We'll travel back together to the store before closing. I have a delivery truck set up with Khaled to get you back into the store. Rand in disguise will be at the store to pick you up to take you to Ibrahim's place. I think SK will make her move someplace on the route between the store and Ibrahim's. Drew and I will be doing recon and tracking you and Rand, and hopefully we can flush SK first."

"Good grief! Rand will be here in twenty minutes and I've got to shower and get ready or I'll be late for work. Keep me posted during the day if anything else breaks. We can meet at the Command Center for supper and go over everything again."

"I'll do the honors of preparing supper. How's Chinese sound?"

"Perfect." Rainey flipped the cover to the cell phone and made a beeline for the shower. No way would she make it on time. Rand would just have to sit out front and wait. She'd blame it on Jonah.

* * *

"Don't you dare say a word about this getup," were the first words out of Rand's mouth.

"What? No good morning Rainey, or some comment about keeping you waiting?" Rainey tried to lighten the mood.

Rand did not reply. He started the engine and backed out of the driveway. "I want you to watch the side mirror and surroundings, Rainey. You see anything at all that looks different or gives you a negative feeling, speak up. Let's stay sharp, okay?" Rand's voice was all business now, and the smile in Raney's voice disappeared.

"Understood, Rand."

Rand pulled into a parking space close to the front doors of the Sultana store and waited.

"Looks okay for Rainey to get out and go into the store," Jonah said.

"Jonah says it looks okay to go into the store, Rainey. Remember, do not leave the store and stay in the front. If you need to go to the back of the store for anything, let Yusuf know. He's got security duty covering the inside back exits to the store."

Rainey took a deep breath and nodded to Rand before getting out of the car. It was hard to act 'normal' with the fear crawling around inside her. Jonah and Rand felt certain SK would make her move tomorrow, but Rainey knew she was unpredictable and they had too little information on which to rule out SK going after a Six-of-Ten target today.

Rainey walked forward toward the store door and breathed a small sigh of relief as the door closed behind her. Her palms were sweating inside her gloves and a trickle of sweat ran down the side of her face underneath the face veil.

"As Salaam'Alaykum, Sister Amira. Are you feeling better today?" Maryam greeted Rainey as she walked towards the book section of the store.

Pausing momentarily, Rainey replied, "Wa 'alaykum as salaam. Alhamdulillah, much better thank you."

"It must be a bug going around. Sister A'aminah called in sick today."

"Allah willing she will recover quickly as I did. I hope I did not give the bug to her."

"She will be fine. Do not concern yourself. A'aminah told me she would be back to work tomorrow. Is there anything I can help you with?" Rainey nodded her head no. "If you need me I will be just three aisles over working in the herbs and spices section today."

"Thanks, Sister Maryam. I appreciate your thoughtfulness." Rainey nodded to several other store employees before shelving the books she began the day before. The day was uneventful for Rainey. She watched the door as patrons came and went, answering customers' questions and shelving a new delivery. Rainey ate lunch with Maryam at a table set up near the stock room and they talked about Maryam's fall classes and Amira's hopes to fit in the community. Rainey felt embarrassed both accepting Maryam's confidences and concocting a false biography that included Amira's plans for school in the fall.

Rand and Jonah were silent except for Rand's communicating that Drew called and was remaining in Los Angles to stay in touch with Lieutenant Jerald, who was now a full working member of the Copy Cat task force, sifting through information and witness statements.

At five o'clock, Rand showed up in costume and parked close to the store entrance. Rainey gave her salaams to co-workers who would be working until the store closed. She waited at the front door until Jonah gave her the all clear. Rainey walked quickly from the store and got into the front passenger seat. Rand nodded and backed out of the space and started the short drive to Ibrahim's place.

"Remember, keep your eyes sharp and be alert. SK could be waiting out there to try and waylay us," Rand reminded Rainey.

She nodded her head, feeling the fear once again that she had managed to push aside during her day at the store.

The ride to Ibrahim's place was uneventful just as the day had been.

"I will drop you off. Stay covered. Several car loads of sisters and brothers are coming to visit Ibrahim. You will leave with one group after a thirty minute visit. Jonah will be waiting along the highway and the driver will pull over and let you out of the vehicle. If SK is watching, she will be watching Ibrahim's place and waiting for you to return to the bungalow from his house. Two of the sisters will go to the bungalow and wait there for you to return tonight. Ibrahim has worked out the details for one of the men to come and get them. You will be in that car and get out as they are getting in the car. Hopefully with Ibrahim making a lot of fuss there will be enough distraction that if SK is watching she won't catch on."

Rainey digested this and tried for a light note. "All this so Jonah can cook supper for me again?"

Rand pulled up to the gate and waited for Rainey to press the locking device so the gate would open. "Jonah doesn't think all this is necessary as he still thinks SK intends to strike tomorrow and not at Ibrahim's place."

"So what do you think, Rand?"

"I think SK is just jerking everyone around. That's what I think."

"Maybe so," Rainey said thoughtfully as she got out of the car. "See you at the Command Center," she said and closed the car door.

Two Muslim brothers were waiting outside their bungalow and hurried to walk Rainey to her front door. She thanked them and went inside breathing a sigh of relief. The tension in her shoulders and neck hit with full force as she sat down and tried to relax for a few minutes.

Rainey went into the restroom and came out just as she heard the cars driving through the gates. "Show time," she said softly. She went out the door and was joined by the brothers in the other bungalow. They walked her to Ibrahim's house. She smiled as she listened to about a dozen Muslim friends greeting each other with salaams.

Breaking News

Monday evening

Rainey sat on one of the benches in the Command Center watching Jonah work putting together their supper. Rand had the television monitors on scanning the news stations. *Does Rand ever relax?* Rainey wondered.

"Big day tomorrow, Rainey. Are you nervous?" Jonah asked.

"Nervous about SK or nervous about having to deal with the task force?" she answered with a question.

"I guess nervous doesn't quite cover either situation, does it?"Jonah responded.

Rainey paused as she was about to respond. A memory from the past seemed to jump out at her. *Sara did that. Fired off one question after another, sometimes not waiting for an answer.* Rainey's eyes suddenly felt teary and she looked away from Jonah.

Jonah noticed and said with concern, "Rainey, what is it? What did I say?"

Before Rainey could say anything Rand spoke. "Rainey. Jonah. Would you look at the brass!" They both looked at Rand's screen setup. Rainey noted that the same six o'clock news story was on all the cable and local stations.

Rainey saw the Los Angeles chief of police, mayor, several council members and a State senator standing behind a podium on the steps of the LAPD in front of a bank of frenzied reporters thrusting mikes at the Chief who was talking. The picture on the monitors cut to two pictures of an older man and a fiftyish younger version of him. The family resemblance was striking. The ticker-tape captions running across the bottom of the screens identified the two men as James E. Thornton, Senior and James E. Thornton II.

The Chief was talking about three brutal slayings and a robbery at the home of the elder Thornton late Sunday evening. The bodies were discovered several hours ago, time non-specific, by LAPD after receiving an anonymous tip. A sixty-seven-year-old butler in the house at the time of the murders was found dead in the kitchen. The deceased were well-known philanthropists and owners of the mega million dollar Thornton Industries with smaller holdings, one of which was a pharmaceutical headquartered in LA. Police were looking for the younger Thomas E. Thornton III, a vice president of the pharmaceutical company. He is presumed missing, as he failed to show up for an important board of directors meeting Monday morning and was not located at his apartment in Thornton Towers.

The report went on to say that an undisclosed police source stated there is concern that harm may have been done to the youngest Thornton family member. There is speculation that he was kidnapped and the unknown killer or killers may attempt to extort money from Thornton business enterprises. The Chief did not comment on this speculation.

Rainey's attention began to fade until Rand let out a loud yell and said, "I'll be a son of a ... Listen to this, you guys."

"Andrea Mitchell of the LA Times. Chief Ballard, Can you confirm that a silver Bentley found abandoned at LAX late this afternoon may be involved in the triple homicide?"

The police chief's face seemed to puff up as he glared at the reporter. "No comment. The homicides are under investigation, and when we have more facts, we will inform the people of Los

Angeles and the press." He and his minions made a quick departure from the podium as a Captain Arnold Miller, Public Affairs Coordinator for the Office of the Chief of Police took the mike now abandoned by the LA dignitaries.

Another reporter was shouting at the Chief of Police's back, asking if there were any leads as to who reported the murders.

Jonah was already dialing Drew. He hung up and dialed again. "No answer," Jonah said somberly. "Something is going down. I can feel it."

Rainey's cell phone rang and she flipped the cover and answered it. She didn't recognize the phone number. "Yes?"

"Rainey, this is Khaled speaking. We have a small problem here at the store. A detective was here asking about a SUV parked in front of our store last evening close to closing time. It seems this SUV is specially equipped for the handicapped. It was stolen from the Bright Days Community yesterday just hours before it was seen parked in front of the store. I know you already left work, but this concerns you and perhaps why you are here."

"How can the theft of this SUV involve me and what I am doing in the community?"

"I will explain more."

"I am sorry Khaled. Please continue."

"The detective asked to talk to Yusuf and Sister Maryam. They closed the store last evening with Sister A'aminah. They did not see this SUV but they told the detective that Sister A'aminah had talked to a customer who came in late. They did not see the customer. The customer left before they came from the back of the store. He wanted to talk to Sister A'aminah, but I explained she was out sick today. He said he wants to interview her tomorrow at nine AM."

"What is your concern?" Rainey asked calmly, though her adrenalin was beginning to pump and she felt the sensation she always got when something significant was about to happen.

"I telephoned Sister A'aminah to tell her about this detective and why he wanted to speak to her. She was very nervous about this detective wanting to talk to her. She told me about an elderly Muslim woman who drove a SUV equipped with a lift and wheelchair for the driver. She said this nice elderly Muslimah talked with her for a few minutes only. The Muslimah had stopped by the store to leave a gift for you. She told Sister A'aminah she had missed you at the masjid and she was leaving town today and would not be able to give the gift to you, so Sister A'aminah accepted the gift for you."

Rainey felt like she had been kicked in the stomach. She said softly, "SK."

"What did Sister A'aminah do with this gift?" Rainey asked Khaled, mustering all her resources not to get him more concerned.

"She said she was going to put it in my office but then she was so busy talking to this old Muslimah that she got behind on her closing jobs. Yusuf told me he had mildly rebuked her and perhaps this is why she did not say anything to Yusuf or Sister Maryam last night about this old woman."

Rainey made herself speak calmly as she asked again, "What did A'aminah do with the gift from the old Muslimah?"

"She took it home with her, intending to bring it to the store today and give it to you, but she became ill. She thought she would give it to you tomorrow. Now she is worried about what to say to this detective and whether she should tell him about the gift the old woman left for you. She doesn't want to have this detective bothering you also."

"Are you sure the detective will wait until tomorrow to interview A'aminah at the store?"

"Oh yes I am sure. He is familiar about how a single Muslimah would be very uncomfortable talking to a male by herself. He was very sensitive, all thanks be to Allah."

"Is A'aminah staying by herself? You are sure she is feeling better?"

"Yes, My good wife has been with her all day so she would have company and see to her needs. After I talked to Sister A'aminah, I drove to her apartment and picked up the old woman's gift. I brought it back to the store. I called Brother Ibrahim to tell you to call me but he told me you were not at the bungalow and he suggested I call you direct as I have done."

"I will come to the store right away. Please call A'aminah and tell her that I will take care of the matter with the detective and she will not need to worry. Ask her to write what she said and the old woman said to the best of her memory and describe the old woman and the SUV she saw. Tell her to sign this and put the date on it. She can bring her statement to the store tomorrow."

"It is a great relief that you will speak to this detective. I thank you for Sister A'aminah. She is a sweet child and so kind. I will wait here at the store until you come for the package."

"Thank you Khaled." Rainey closed the cover of the phone and looked up to see Rand and Jonah staring at her.

"I can't say for sure but we will soon know. I think SK smelled the trap. She has been here and I think she is gone." Her bitterness and frustration resonated in her voice and the welling tears of anger were hard for Rainey to control. They had failed, again. All the planning. They had been spinning their wheels and getting no place.

Jonah and Rand listened intently as Rainey repeated what Khaled had said. In one motion the three of them began clearing the table and getting the Command Center ready to roll.

"My vote is we drive to the store, pick up the package, and get started for LA." Rand said.

"And what about the Brantlie PD, Detective? We just can't leave Khaled and everyone at the store being grilled and unable to talk freely."

"Let's get to the store and Rainey can see what is inside the package. After that we decide whether we talk to the detective or get another cop to talk to him. Rainey, why don't you call Ibrahim and ask him to meet us at the store?"

"Good idea, Jonah." Rainey flipped open her cell phone and dialed Ibrahim.

"I think after we find out what's inside the package I will call DC. If we need a heavy hitter to watch our backside and deal with the Brantlie PD he's our best and only choice."

Jonah and Rand raised their eyebrows.

"His bark is worse than his bite. We didn't do anything that can be construed as illegal and we didn't mess with the LAPD task force's investigation of the Copy Cat. SK is the one who has been manipulating all of us."

Rand and Jonah didn't respond to Rainey's comments about DC Britt. Rainey straightened her shoulders and chose to ignore them.

"Jonah, did you try Drew's number again?" Rand asked.

"Yes, I've called six times with no response. I placed three calls to Bob Jerald and he's not answering his cell phone either."

Jonah took the driver's seat in the Command Center and they began the short drive to the Sultana Books & More Store.

Saying Goodbye

Monday evening

Jonah pulled the Command Center into a parking space close to the front of the store. Jonah, Rand, and Rainey walked into the store. Rainey, dressed in non-Muslim clothing, went unrecognized by employees as the three made their way to the rear of the store, where Khaled and Ibrahim waited anxiously in the doorway that led to the back rooms. They walked quickly after the two Muslim men to Khaled's office. Khaled waited until everyone was inside before he closed the door. He offered Rainey a chair, motioned to the men to have a seat on the couch, and sat down behind his desk.

Khaled picked up a rectangle shaped package that was wrapped in brown paper and held it out to Rainey.

Rainey noted that the package's dimensions were similar to a book, and the package felt and weighed like a book. The only writing on the package was the name "Amira." The package was sealed with what looked like common scotch tape at the two ends and down the seam where the brown paper overlapped.

Rainey passed the package to Rand who looked at it carefully and handed it to Jonah. Jonah looked at the package and then handed it back to Rainey.

"If I were a cop I would consider this package a piece of evidence," Rainey said to no one in particular. When no one answered, Rainey turned the package in her hands once again and then placed it on a corner of Khaled's desk.

"Is now the time we invite the Brantlie PD to join us?"

"We don't know for sure that the package is from SK," Rand said.

"It could be just a gift from an old woman," Jonah commented.

Khaled and Ibrahim had sat silently watching the three non-Muslims discuss the package.

Ibrahim cleared his throat and the other four people in the room looked at him. "If this old woman is SK and she stole the SUV from the retirement community, wouldn't the package be considered evidence?"

"Yes, Ibrahim. The police will consider it evidence." Rainey replied.

"Right now I think the Brantlie Chief of Police would be upset that we set up our *operation* and didn't tell him anything, but we haven't broken any laws. If Rainey opens the package and then we withhold it from the police, we would all be breaking the law," Rand commented.

"What if Rainey as Amira opens the package first to find out what it is and if it is just a gift from an old woman then we would have no reason to tell the police anymore than this," Jonah suggested.

"Call it intuition or whatever, but I feel certain the package is from SK," Rainey said.

Jonah looked at Rainey's intense expression and considered her words. "Then we have little choice but to call the police and you'll have to open the package in front of the police and whatever is inside we will have to explain to the detective or chief."

"Maybe now would be a good time for me to call DC and let him run interference for me? If SK has left me another note then it will probably have something to do with the Copy Cat killer as well, and that means notifying the LAPD Task Force. I'd rather

DC Britt soften them up before I have to talk to the task force commander."

"I think this is a good idea," Khaled offered, and Ibrahim nodded his head in agreement. Rainey looked at Rand and then Jonah. Both nodded their heads in agreement, too.

"I suggest that Rainey wear the communications device and wait here with Khaled and Ibrahim for the Brantlie police to arrive. Rand and I will make ourselves scarce. We will be able to hear what you say and pick up most of whatever else is said in this room."

"I'll call DC now, and then Khaled can call the police and ask for the detective to come to the store."

"Sounds like a plan to me," Rand said.

Rainey looked at Khaled and pointed to the phone on his desk, "May I?"

"Yes go ahead. There is a speaker phone function you might want to use. We could all hear the conversation," Khaled suggested.

Rainey nodded and Khaled pushed the button. Rainey dialed DC's office number.

"DC Britt."

"DC, it's Rainey."

"Making a habit of evening calls are you?" DC said sarcastically.

Rainey ignored DC's tone of voice and plunged right in. "DC, I am in Brantlie, California. I have some things to tell you, and I need your help." Without waiting for DC's response, Rainey told him about the SK operation and the package.

DC listened without interrupting until Rainey requested that he telephone the Chief of Police in Brantlie. "When you open the package in the presence of the chief or one of his detectives, and if it is from SK, I want your word you will call me immediately. Not hours from now or tomorrow. Am I making that clear to you, Rainey?"

"Yes, I understand and agree." Rainey said in her most humble tone of voice.

"If the package is from SK, I'll call the LAPD Task force commander and let him know to expect you in LA within the next couple of hours. I think I can persuade the Chief to release the package to your custody. You'll have to turn it over to the task force. Agreed?"

Rainey felt a flood of relief and swallowed hard before replying. "Agreed."

"Just sit tight and wait to hear from the Brantlie police." DC said next.

"I'll wait here at the store with the store owner and also the imam of the local masjid."

"And Rainey, if Jonah and his associates just happen to be in Brantlie, California they would be wise to make immediate travel plans." DC broke the phone connection.

The four men stood and shook hands. Rainey felt a pang as Jonah and Rand walked out the door. She knew they would be in the vicinity but facing the Chief of Police or a detective without their support was something Rainey had not contemplated when she had devised this SK operation just a week ago. So much had happened in such a short time. Her disappointment in the failure of the operation left a bitter taste in her mouth.

"Ibrahim and Khaled I am so sorry. It seems the Echo investigators and I have failed your community. I don't know how SK was able to determine I am here as Amira, but she did."

"We do not find this outcome a failure. She could not get at you as Amira and she knows the Muslim community is not sleeping. All is as Allah wills and we are thankful no one in our community has been harmed and you and the men helping are unharmed as well," Ibrahim replied.

"Would you like a cup of tea or coffee, Rainey while we wait?" Khaled offered.

"Coffee would be good. Thank you." The coffee would give her something to do with her hands. She wanted desperately to rip off the brown paper and see what SK had left for her. Whatever it was, she knew it would include SK's particular brand of sick thinking.

Christopher Carrington – Copy Cat
Monday night

Jonah moved the RV a block away from the Sultana store, but still well within the limitations of the communications device he and Rainey were using.

His cell phone rang. Jonah answered with "Echo."

"It's Drew. Sorry I've been out of touch. Are Rainey and Rand there with you? The task force thinks it has the location of the Copy Cat killer and tactical is in its war room making a plan to take him down"

"Hold on a sec, Drew."

Jonah took the communications device out of his ear and handed it to Rand. "I need to tell Drew what's happened and he told me the task force is preparing to take the Copy Cat down." Rand took the device with raised eyebrows, but did not comment.

"Drew, I need to tell you want has happened here in Brantlie. The SK operation is blown."

"How did that go down, Jonah?"

Jonah briefed Drew and when he was through he heard Drew give a low whistle. "Man, if that doesn't suck. Bob Jerald is gonna be pissed. How's Rainey holding up?"

"I'll know more how she is once she opens that package we believe SK left for her. It could be anything, but we know it won't be good," Jonah replied.

"I wonder what clued SK in to the operation."

"Rainey said something the other day and it kind of stuck with me. Rand wondered how SK always knew so much about what was going on and where people were. Rainey said that it's possible that SK is better at seeing the obvious while most of us don't."

"You mean something along the lines, if it's too good to be true then it's not? Like the article in the Muslim newspaper about the Muslim niece from Iraq coming to the US and staying with her uncle and aunt. Planning on attending school and working part time in the store in Brantlie."

"Right. If SK had been hunting for months and couldn't find any victims fitting her unique criteria and then one just materializes out of nowhere....."

"There you have it...the obvious weakness in the plan that we didn't see," Drew said.

"What bothers me is how she got around all our security... moved around in the town and we didn't have a clue. When this is all over we are going to have a debriefing and go over every single thing Echo did in the operation," Jonah said.

"I agree."

"You said the LAPD task force and tactical is getting ready to close in on the Copy Cat. How'd that come about?"

"Did you watch any news earlier today? There was a story about a double homicide of two big wigs and at the end of the press conference, one reporter mentioned something about an abandoned silver Bentley at the airport being linked to the killings."

"Yeah. Rand picked up on it. He remembered about Copy Cat's fourth kill and one of the witnesses at the Waldorf Hotel saying some guy was driving a silver Bentley and at the hotel at that time. Bob Jerald told you the detectives were looking for the owners of registered Bentleys in the LA and surrounding areas to find a potential witness."

"Right. When the PD impounded the abandoned Bentley, they took it to their impound lot for the CSI to go over. It was a dead end, at first. The CSI went over the Bentley with a fine tooth comb. In the trunk, they found a single earring that looked like it had an authentic gem stone in it, but they didn't find a single fingerprint—not even a partial. The car had been wiped clean."

"That's enough to raise suspicion," Jonah said.

"Well, the thing is, the registered owner came back to a Harold Carrington, deceased two years ago. No record of the Bentley being sold or reregistered. They wrote it off as some reporter trying to make news when there wasn't any story."

"Something change the dead-end status of the Bentley?" Jonah asked.

"About two hours ago a woman calls the Copy Cat hotline and identifies herself as a secretary working for Thorndyne Pharmaceuticals. She says a previous employee, an accountant, owned a silver Bentley that his father left him when the father died. She told the hotline that this man quit about six months ago with no advanced notice. Get this. He sent in an email resignation. She goes on to say that this accountant was a friend of Thomas E. Thornton III. They use to work out in the gym together. Both good looking guys similar in height and build. She said Carrington was a quiet but friendly guy. This Thornton guy though, is a horse of a different color. Secretary said to keep that info confidential."

"Isn't that the Thornton that is missing? The one they flashed his photo in the news with the same story reporting his grandfather and father being killed in a robbery-homicide at the grandfather's home last night?"

"One and the same. The LAPD went to the penthouse of the youngest Thornton to give the death notification this afternoon. The doorman told the cops that Thornton ordered his car to be ready at eight AM today as he had an important meeting to attend. The doorman sent the valet to get the car but then Thornton never came down from his apartment. The front desk called his room but he didn't answer. The manager said he was concerned. He told the cops that Thornton had been sick all day Sunday and had mentioned he would not be able to attend a dinner that evening at his grandfather's home."

"Lucky guy," Jonah commented.

"Maybe not so lucky. The manager and the two cops went to the penthouse apartment and the manager let the cops in. Everything looked okay except Thornton wasn't in the apartment, and he was a no show at the Thorndyne Pharmaceuticals Board of Directors meeting earlier in the morning."

"So that's why he's been reported as missing?"

"Right."

"So the LAPD now has a link between a former employee of Thorndyne owning a Bentley and the Thorntons, and a possible link to the Copy Cat's fourth kill at the Waldorf through the Bentley?"

"The secretary looked up the last known address of the accountant. His name, by the way, is Christopher Carrington. I thought it was just me, but Jerald picked up on the name, too. The accountant's initials are the same as the initials for 'Copy Cat.' C. C."

Jonah didn't comment.

"The TF commander decided to send a LAPD homicide detective and a task force sergeant to this address for Christopher Carrington. The guy doesn't answer his phone or door. The cops left their business cards stuck on the door and called it in to the commander.

"Jerald called me and says we need a fast meet at that restaurant three blocks from the PD. The one where SK left that package for him and Rainey. He told me that all the airlines were checked to see if this Carrington guy left LA, but he didn't purchase a ticket in his own name. The cops took a photo of him they got from the personnel files at Thorndyne and showed it around at the various airlines at LAX, but didn't get anyone to say they had seen him or sold a ticket to someone who looked like him."

"He could have disguised his appearance or someone on a different shift might have seen him," Jonah said.

"That's possible. Captain Jenkins doesn't buy his leaving LA. He thinks Carrington is holed up in his apartment and is holding the missing Thornton hostage."

"Doesn't sound likely that a serial killer would do that, but if he feels cornered, he might do anything. Serial killers are unpredictable. But why leave the Bentley at the airport? Trying to throw the cops off his trail? Things are just not adding up. This whole case is a cluster!"

"Right now everyone is on standby. Captain Jenkins is in with a judge trying to get a search warrant signed for Carrington's apartment. I don't think he'll have much of a problem although Jerald says the PC is a little thin… based on lots of assumptions, so Jenkins is using exigent circumstances."

"'If his approach is a hostage-type situation that means evacuating other tenants. What kind of structure?"

"It's gonna be a bitch. His apartment is on the tenth floor. They'll have to evacuate at least a couple of floors above and below Carrington's apartment. It's in an upscale yuppie type complex."

Rand pulled on Jonah's sleeve. "Hold on Drew. Rand needs to tell me something. He's in communications with Rainey."

"Rainey wanted to talk with you, Jonah. She's going to try and call again when she's not under police scrutiny. The package was from SK. She wrote Rainey another note. Apologized for standing Rainey up tomorrow and gave her the name of the killer. Said the LAPD was to inept to figure things out, so she did the job for them. I'll let her tell you more about the package when she calls you. If Drew is still on the line, tell him that SK said Christopher Carrington is the C.C. Rainey and the Brantlie Police Chief have left for LA, and DC Britt called Captain Jenkins and he's expecting them."

Jonah relayed Rainey's information to Drew and told him to call him back if anything changed.

While waiting for Rainey's call, Jonah filled Rand in on what was happening in LA. Jonah felt useless and tense sitting around waiting for phone calls. He could see Rand was getting antsy, too.

"How about we blow this burg and head for LA?"

Rand gave Jonah a slow grin. "You don't have to ask twice. Let's move."

Gotcha!

Monday night

Rainey sat quietly in the front passenger seat of Chief Garcia's unmarked police vehicle. On the seat between them was an evidence bag with SK's package. Chief Garcia was not talking to her. The atmosphere inside the vehicle was below zero. After his initial lecture and harsh words of censure, the Chief literally ignored Rainey.

Rainey needed to talk to Jonah, but was not going to do so in the presence of the Chief. It would have to wait until she got a moment alone once they got to the LAPD. Rainey was glad about one thing. The Chief told Ibrahim and Khaled that the stolen SUV with the disability setup was found abandoned by CHIPS about a half mile from a motel seven miles north of Brantlie. An abeya, head scarf, gloves and veil were left in the driver's seat. The Chief speculated that SK had been staying at the motel. One of his detectives was at the motel interviewing the owners and employees.

She had spoken briefly to Captain Jenkins and was pleasantly surprised when he didn't berate or give her hell. He listened and said he would be waiting for her arrival. He told her the plan was in progress to do a search on Carrington's apartment. The task force and tactical team were en route and he was leaving the office with Lieutenant Jerald. He told the Chief when they got to LA to call him and he'd direct them to the apartment complex where the search was going to be done. That was all he said. Rainey was surprised, yet still anxious.

Did the Copy Cat get away? Did SK and the Copy Cat meet? Did one or both survive? Rainey had a feeling that what they were going to find in the apartment would be horrible if SK made good her threat to take out the Copy Cat before she blew town.

The Chief made the two-hour drive in a little over an hour. He pulled to the side of the road and called Captain Jenkins.

"The Captain said to bring you to the crime scene."

"Okay," was all Rainey could manage to say. The Chief didn't invite any conversation.

Twenty minutes later they turned onto Beverly Avenue and saw the police barricades and yellow crime scene tape. Crowds of onlookers were standing around craning their necks trying to see what the cops were doing. The CSI van was parked in front of the building as was the black station wagon marked LA County Coroner. Dozens of cops in standard uniform or in flak vests and jumpsuits were busy keeping the onlookers away from the building. The building was a fifteen story high rise with a modern architectural design.

The chief pulled up to the barricade stretched across the street and a LAPD cop approached. The Chief rolled down his window and showed his badge to the cop. "Captain Jenkins is expecting me and the woman passenger." was all he said.

"Sir if you'll stay in your vehicle and wait I'll contact Captain Jenkins." The cop walked a few feet away and Rainey could see him speaking into the mike attached to his shirt collar. She looked around at the crowd and spotted a tall man with a face she recognized. *Drew.*

"Hey, Ms. Walker. Where do you think you're going?" the Chief yelled as Rainey opened the passenger door and got out of the car. She slammed the door while the Chief was still yelling at her. In a few seconds, she disappeared from sight within the crowd.

Drew tracked her progress through the crowd and gently pulled on her arm when he caught up to her, guiding her to an alleyway between two buildings across the street from the apartment complex.

"Am I glad to see you, Drew. I am not sure if that Chief of Police from Brantlie considers me under arrest or not. He sure acts like it. If I had to sit another minute with him in that car, I was going to scream."

"I take it the Chief wasn't too happy about our little operation in his city?" Drew's eyes twinkled and he smiled warmly at Rainey.

Relieved, Rainey smiled back at Drew and a huge weight seemed to dissolve from around her shoulders.

"I heard Captain Jenkins tell the Chief that he was out at a crime scene. Could we be lucky enough for the victim to be SK?"

"Fraid not, Rainey. The victim is definitely male, but Bob texted me and said they are not sure if the body is Christopher Carrington or James Thornton."

"Did the LAPD take him down or..."

"Jerald said the coroner placed a tentative time of death between midnight and six o'clock this morning. He couldn't be more specific until he gets the body back and does the autopsy."

Rainey digested this information and a thought hit her. "If the body was DOA and male, it's definitely not SK. I don't know Carrington or Thornton. I could have left the evidence from SK at the LAPD. Why would Captain Jenkins insist I come to this crime scene?"

"I don't know, Rainey. Bob came out about twenty minutes ago and said the body inside the apartment was butchered. Blood everywhere. The killer shot him in both knee caps and broke both arms. The victim was stretched spread eagle on the carpet and his hands were pinned to the carpet with knives driven through the palms. The coroner said the victim was breathing when that was done."

Raney shuddered and said softly, "My God."

"It gets worse. Each of the victim's fingers were sliced off with a very sharp instrument and all eight fingers and the two thumbs were placed on his stomach. The bastard was alive when that happened."

Rainey's stomach lurched when she heard this description. "Drew, tell me the guy died without any further torture."

"Torture is the best description for what was done to him. What caused his death was a syringe and needle stuck in his right eye jammed clear through to the brain."

Rainey shuddered again.

"Now comes the key to the killer's identity. The killer left a Post-it note stuck to the victim's forehead. It said, 'Adios,' a dash, followed by the signature, Es Que."

"She's still out there, Drew!" Rainey knew this deep inside when she opened the package, which contained a signed book and a personal letter. The author of both was her grandmother, who had given the book to Rainey years ago. Rainey thought the book and everything else she owned had been lost when SK had bombed her home last year. It made Rainey anxious and angry, thinking that SK had her hands on her property. The book she returned to Rainey was the last book in her grandmother's series and was titled, *Saying Goodbye*. SK was a sick psycho and was apparently fixated on Rainey.

"Rainey, I see Captain Jenkins standing at the Chief's car talking to him. He is scanning the crowd. If you want to know why you're at this crime scene, you better go talk to Captain Jenkins. I need to call Jonah and tell him about this. He and Rand are on their way to LA to pick me up. We'll be going back to the East Coast. I'll call or Jonah will later tonight or you call us when you get a chance to get away from the cops for some privacy." Drew squeezed Rainey's shoulder and bent down and brushed his lips on her forehead. "Go get 'em, girl."

As Drew stepped back, Rainey reached out and pulled gently on the sleeve of his jacket. "Drew do you think you can hang out here a bit longer. Wait for me?"

"Sure Rainey. No problem. Just call or text me when you're clear."

Rainey moved diagonally from where Drew faded back into the alleyway and then she moved through the crowd and walked up to the two cops.

Rainey extended her arm and said, "I'm Rainey Walker. You wanted me to come to this crime scene, Captain Jenkins?"

Captain Jenkins shook Rainey's proffered hand and said, "Ms. Walker. It is good to meet you at last. Thanks for bringing the evidence. The information you provided was the probable cause that fortified my application for our search warrant."

"Did you find your Copy Cat killer, Captain Jenkins?"

"Yes, Ms Walker, we did and then some. We found a trunk full of his trophies in crystal jars like the one the SK sent to Lieutenant Jerald and you. I'll go into details later. Right now I need for you to come with me. We found something that will interest you and involves you. It is in another apartment on the eighth floor. I think it will make more sense for you to see the room and I'd like to get your own first impressions rather than me try to explain. Do you have any reservations with accompanying me?"

"No problem for me. Lead the way."

The Captain and Rainey rode the elevator to the eighth floor and stepped out. Rainey saw two uniformed LAPD police officers standing outside the closed door to apartment 802. The Captain nodded to the two officers and they smiled at Rainey. One of them opened the door and Rainey and the Captain stepped inside.

Rainey looked at the tall, wide-shouldered man standing in the middle of the living room with an anxious look on his face.

"Lieutenant Jerald." Rainey spoke his name softly. A flash of pain crossed her face as she saw him in the hospital again back in

Arizona holding her cold hands and telling her what she did not want to hear.

Bob Jerald stood silently waiting, his eyes pleading. Rainey took a step forward and Bob seemed not to know what to say or do. He just waited.

Rainey looked at this big lug of a cop and the ice around her heart seemed to thaw. She walked swiftly forward and put her arms around him and hugged him. Bob stood stiffly at first and then realizing that Rainey was no longer angry, he smiled and stepped back slightly.

"Ah... Rainey Walker, it is so good to see you again." He knew that things were going to be okay now.

"Me, too," Rainey answered and wiped the silent tears from her eyes.

Captain Jenkins had stood silently watching Rainey and Lieutenant Jerald. What had just happened was not something he understood. Both Lieutenant Jerald and Rainey Walker seemed to have changed in front of his eyes. *There was a story here. Maybe Jerald would tell him some time?*

Captain Jenkins cleared his throat and both Rainey and Bob looked at him. "What I brought you here for is in the bedroom. If you'd like to take a look now."

Lieutenant Jerald handed Rainey a pair of gloves and paper shoe covers to wear to protect the crime scene. Rainey pulled them on and entered the bedroom. At first glance nothing seemed out of the ordinary. There was a queen size bed neatly made, flanked by night stands and lamps, and a six-drawer dresser. The closet was open and almost empty. Rainey looked at the overstuffed chair in one corner of the room. A silver and purple jump suit with orange flames imprinted on the fabric was thrown carelessly over the back of the chair. A matching biker helmet was on the chair seat and a pair of black biker boots was on the floor in front of the chair.

Bob Jerald, standing behind Rainey said, "There is a Yamaha 650 parked in underground garage space assigned to this apartment and it is painted exactly like that jump suit." Rainey looked back over her shoulder and raised an eyebrow but didn't comment.

She scanned the room, noticing something laying on the center of the bed. As she approached the bed, she saw what looked like the back of a photograph with her name written in block letters. Next to the overturned photograph was a letter-sized envelope with her name printed neatly on it.

Rainey's hand trembled as she bent forward, stretched her arm and flipped over the photograph. Staring back at Rainey was a picture of her dressed as Amira and standing in the Book Section of the Sultana Books & More Store. At the top of the photo SK had written one word, GOTCHA!

Rainey sat down on the edge of the bed. *How did she know? When did she take the photo? It had to have been Sunday...just yesterday.* Sunday seemed like such a long time ago as she looked at the photograph of herself.

With a quaver to her voice Rainey asked, "Has anyone read the letter she left for me?"

Captain Jenkins had moved into the room and was standing beside Lieutenant Jerald. "No Rainey, we flipped the picture as you did, but we left the letter just as SK placed it."

"You know she's gone? She's not in Los Angeles anymore." Rainey asked without looking at either of the cops or expecting an answer.

"Okay if I open the letter now?" Rainey looked at Captain Jenkins.

"That's the main reason I wanted you to come here. There's one more thing, Rainey. SK leased this apartment using her own name, Elaine Stewart. She wanted to make sure there were no mistakes about who took out the Copy Cat."

Who is the Copy Cat? Is it Christopher Carrington or James Thornton? Do the cops know now for sure? Rainey shook her head at SK's sheer arrogance. She picked up the envelope and carefully opened the flap. It wasn't sealed.

There was one sheet of paper inside. Rainey recognized SK's cursive writing. It was from her and no one else. Rainey read the letter and then read it a second time out loud.

Rainey,

Are you surprised? After I said goodbye in Brantlie and here I am in LA, like a bad penny turning up again. Ha!

That outfit in your photo is most unbecoming. Really you need to improve your fashion sense.

Did you see my latest handiwork? I was surprised at how tough Copy Cat was. Hard to believe he suffered such torment just to protect his precious secret. He knew I would never leave him alive. I solved the crime for LAPD. Just as inept as the Phoenix PD. But you and I know this. Have they figured out that James Thornton is their copy-cat? If not you must set them straight. I put too much time into doing their job to have them screw it up.

Now to the reason Jimmy-boy fought nearly until the end, but he broke. Christopher Carrington is alive. He and Jimmy-boy were lovers. I mean weird or what. A serial killer with a heart. Jimmy-boy sent him to the French Rivera to wait for him. Carrington's new persona is...

I think I'll leave it for another time. Maybe I'll visit the Rivera and look ol' Chris up? What do you think Rainey?

Jimmy-boy got exactly what he deserved. I had to take months away from my mission to put a stop to him. He ruined any chance I would find my Six-of-Ten in LA or almost anyplace in California. AND I will find Six-of-Ten and the other four heathens who deserve to die. I will finish my mission. Stay out of my way, Rainey Walker. This time I let you skate. You did nothing to deter me. This time it was James Thornton and his ill conceived Copy Cat and you see what price he paid. I can promise the same or worse if you continue interfering. Next time you will not be so lucky. SK.

Rainey placed SK's letter back in the envelope and put it back on the bed with the picture for the CSI Team to collect as evidence. She looked up at Captain Jenkins and asked, "Does the apartment complex have cameras installed?"

"Yes. The manager said the tapes are recycled every three months. I've asked the manager to collect the tapes and give them to the task force commander. We'll be checking the security tapes at Thornton Towers as well. Our techs will get photos made from the tapes of SK and Lt. Jerald can get you copies. At least you'll know what she looks like today."

"I appreciate that, but don't know if the photos from the tapes will help much. SK's a master at disguise in whatever persona she wants to use."

Captain Jenkins didn't answer immediately. It looked like he was weighing what he intended to say next. "I learned a little about what you and that Echo Team were doing up in Brantlie. SK is a dangerous adversary. Some friendly advice, Ms. Walker. It would be best if you let let law enforcement handle SK."

"I hear you, Captain Jenkins, but as you just heard what I read from SK's latest letter to me, there is no way I can go about my life ignoring her existence. She's not about to allow me to do that regardless of her warning in that letter."

Epilog

It was after midnight and Rainey, Bob Jerald, and the Echo Team sat at a table in the back of a small bar a few blocks from the crime scene. The bar maid didn't raise an eyebrow when everyone ordered bottled water. They stayed over an hour discussing SK and the gruesome crime scene she created.

They were exhausted and there didn't seem much of anything the five had to celebrate. They were back to square one. They had failed again and SK was gone. When she would surface and where was a huge unknown.

"What did DC Britt say when you called and updated him about what happened here in LA?" Drew asked.

Rainey smiled. "He offered me my job back with the FBI. I turned him down and he hung up on me. He'll cool off and call me back on some pretext just to keep the lines of communications open between us."

"Are you sure you don't want to drive back to New York with Echo, Rainey? We'd love to share your company and you have another week before you leave for Peru," Jonah asked.

"Thanks, but I've decided to fly back to Phoenix and spend a few days with my friends there. Then I'll fly to New York. I'm undecided now about Peru."

"I have to hang around another day to attend the task force debriefing. I have plane reservations for Phoenix for Wednesday afternoon. How about taking a day to rest and then flying back to Phoenix with me on Wednesday?" Bob turned and looked at Rainey.

"Thanks for asking, Bob, but I made a flight reservation already. My plane leaves at two o'clock later today. I could use a lift to the Embassy Suites. The hotel is about fifteen minutes from LAX. I booked one of those business commuter flights to Phoneix Sky Harbor and have a reservation for a week at the Mission Palms in Tempe. I'm going to try and sleep a few hours before my flight. I'm anxious to get back to Phoenix." Rainey smiled at the men seated with her. "If you gentlemen will excuse me, I need to visit the ladies room." Rainey stood and all four men stood up and watched as she headed towards the restroom.

"I wonder what they'll find at Thornton's penthouse apartment." Rand said to no one in particular as the men sat back down to wait for Rainey's return.

"I can answer that question," Bob Jerald replied. "Captain Jenkins sent a couple of task force members and the CSI team to process it. The officers that went to the apartment earlier to give Thornton the death notification of his family didn't find him or anything of significance and neither did the CSI Team. The report is that the apartment is cold, almost sterile. What is curious, maybe significant, is that they didn't find any personal papers or his personal notebook computer."

"Do you think this Carrington guy had anything to do with any of the killings?" Jonah asked.

"I don't know and neither does Captain Jenkins. That's why LAPD won't close the case until they locate him. Besides, they have those twelve jars with body parts belonging to unknown victims that Captain Jenkins says he's not going to give up trying to identify," Bob replied.

"It was decent of Captain Jenkins to give Rainey the book SK sent her. I mean, its evidence. He even got that grump, Chief Garcia, to agree," Drew said.

"I was surprised when he told me he'd have copies of both SK letters to Rainey and some photos of SK ready for me and said he'd see to it that the Copy Cat files were copied so I could take them back to Phoenix."

"I guess us cops and ex-cops are making some progress when it comes to sharing information," Rainey said as she rejoined the men at the table.

"Maybe LAPD should consider hiring Echo to do an investigation into Christopher Carrington? The Echo partners have a lot of overseas contacts and experience." Rainey looked around the table trying hard to suppress a slow grin spreading across her lovely face.

The men said almost in unison, "What are you thinking, Rainey Walker?"

"If SK takes it into her head to go to France to hunt Muslim ten-count victims and decides to look up Christopher Carrington, maybe the Echo team should think about taking some down time on the French Riviera?"

"You mean we act and not react? We go after her and not wait?" Jonah asked.

Rainey shrugged her shoulders and didn't reply as she stood, signaling it was time to leave. Rainey and the four men stood on the sidewalk in front of the bar. She looked at the frowns on the faces of the Echo team, but didn't say anything.

"We'll call you when we decide what our next move is," Jonah said to Rainy as the three Echo partners turned from her and started walking toward Drew's rental car parked a short distance from where Rainey and Bob Jerald stood looking after Echo.

* * *

Bob pulled up in front of the Embassy Suites Hotel and gently shook Rainey's shoulder. She had fallen into a light doze on the drive from the bar.

Rainey yawned and opened her eyes. As she opened the passenger door she said, "That was a short trip. Thanks Bob. No need to get out of the car. When you get back to Phoenix, give me a call. Let's try to have lunch or dinner before I fly back to New York."

"I'll call you. Have a safe flight." Bob replied. He watched as Rainey went through the lobby doors and approached the hotel desk clerk before heading out of the parking lot for his own motel.

The insistent ringing of the phone woke Rainey. She looked at the dial on her wrist watch. *Five o'clock in the morning! I told the night clerk I needed a wakeup call at nine*, she groused as she reached to pick up the receiver and give the person calling a less than polite greeting.

Before she could speak she heard a familiar voice. "Rainey. Jonah, here. Drew and I are at LAX. We just made reservations to fly to New York and catch a flight to France. The New York flight departs in two hours. I'm at the reservation counter now and there is another seat available. Do I book a flight for you?"

"Jonah, when SK is ready to come after me she will. She knows where I live and she all but promised we'd meet again. I think I'll pass on that vacation on the French Rivera, but thanks for asking. You and Drew watch your backs."

"You take care, Rainey Walker."

Rainey heard the click and then the dial tone. She slowly replaced the receiver and closed her eyes. She tried, but failed to go back to sleep. Instead of the sleep she craved, Rainey sat up in the bed and watched the moving minute hand on her watch. She was torn between joining the pursuit of SK and her instincts for self-preservation.

The Author

L.D. Alan retired as a Sergeant in 2000 after a twenty-six year career in law enforcement. The author lives in the Southwest, USA and enjoys writing and spending time with family and friends.

Visit the Rainey Walker Series blog at:
www.raineywalkerseries.wordpress.com

You can write the author at raylin@q.com